ALSO BY SAMANTHA GILLISON

*The Undiscovered Country*

# THE KING
# OF AMERICA

SAMANTHA GILLISON

# THE KING
# OF AMERICA

A NOVEL

RANDOM HOUSE

NEW YORK

All rights reserved under International and Pan-American Copyright Conventions. Published in the United States by Random House, an imprint of The Random House Publishing Group, a division of Random House, Inc., New York, and simultaneously in Canada by Random House of Canada Limited, Toronto.

RANDOM HOUSE and colophon are registered trademarks of Random House, Inc.

Frontispiece photograph courtesy of The Metropolitan Museum of Art, The Michael C. Rockefeller Memorial Collection, Gift of Nelson A. Rockefeller and Mrs. C. Rockefeller, 1965. (1978.412.1248-50) Museum photography; not shown in situ. All rights reserved, The Metropolitan Museum of Art.

Library of Congress Cataloging-in-Publication Data

Gillison, Samantha.
The king of America : a novel / Samantha Gillison.
p. cm.
ISBN 0-375-50819-8
1. Antiquities—Collection and preservation—Fiction. 2. Children of divorced parents—Fiction. 3. Americans—New Guinea—Fiction. 4. Anthropology students—Fiction. 5. Children of the rich—Fiction. 6. Indigenous peoples—Fiction. 7. College students—Fiction. 8. Headhunters—Fiction. 9. New Guinea—Fiction. I. Title.

PS3557.I3945K56 2004
813'.54—dc21          2003046690

Random House website address: www.atrandom.com

Printed in the United States of America on acid-free paper

24689753

First Edition

*For Henry*

# CONTENTS

NORTH
VIETNAM

SOUTH
VIETNAM

Manila

Saigon

PHILIPPINES

*MALAYA*

Singapore

*Equator*

*SUMATRA*

*BORNEO*

*CELEBES*

I N D O N E S I A

Djakarta

*JAVA*

*TIMOR*
(Indonesia)

*EAST
TIMOR*
(Portugal)

*I N D I A N   O C E A N*

A   U

*100° E*

*120° E*

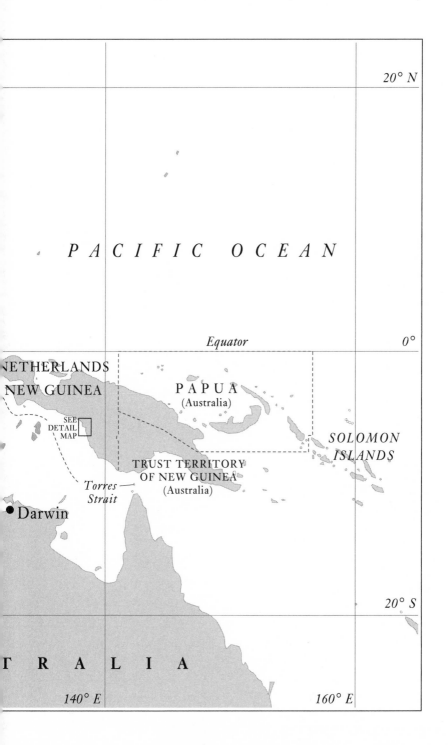

20° N

PACIFIC OCEAN

Equator                                                    0°

NETHERLANDS
NEW GUINEA

PAPUA
(Australia)

SEE
DETAIL
MAP

SOLOMON
ISLANDS

TRUST TERRITORY
OF NEW GUINEA
(Australia)

Torres
Strait

●Darwin

20° S

TRALIA

140° E                                        160° E

# BOOK 1

*So, I turned to consider wisdom and madness*

*and folly; for what can the man do who comes*

*after the king?*

—ECCLESIASTES 2:12

# 1

# THE ARAFURA SEA

A T THE END OF NOVEMBER THE MONSOON BURSTS OVER THE southern coast of Irian Jaya, pounding the villages of thatch-roof huts that sit along the Asmat River. Brackish, cloudy streams that run like veins through the salt swamps swell and then, pulled by the tide, gush muddy, debris-filled water into the shallow Arafura Sea. The air, full of rain, becomes heavy with an earthy, briny smell of rotting shrimp and salt water.

The Arafura is a wide, warm sea that stretches from the southern shore of Irian Jaya down to northern Australia. To its west lie the islands of Indonesia; to the east, across the endless open Pacific, sit Fiji and the New Hebrides. And right before the monsoon hits, its waves become lead-colored, silty, bobbing with branches and tangled roots and the twisted leaves of nipa palms. Flying south from the coast in a low plane, the sea spreads out beneath you, murky, until suddenly, ten miles out from land, the water becomes clear; its rippled sandy bottom glows bluish green in the equatorial sun. And far away from shore the clear water teems with silvery clouds of mackerel, darting eels, and schools of nurse sharks that flicker blue and gray as they make for open ocean.

In November, as the monsoon hovers, the Asmat villagers never travel out that far. They stay close to the coast, paddling long dugout canoes with carved heads guarding their prows. But the American art collector had been in a hurry, eager to get to Agats ahead of the rains: he still hoped to get back to the States for Christmas.

They had gone too far from the shore, Stephen Hesse and the Dutch anthropologist Erich Van Gropius and their two Asmat guides, in the lashed-together catamaran with its tin roof and little outboard motor put-putting in the choppy waves.

It was only early afternoon: the fat, too-close sun still sat high, bleeding haze through the rainy-season clouds. The waves were full of the coming monsoon's violence; one smashed into the other. A huge wave hit the catamaran and swamped the motor. The four men, still sitting in the boat, drifted seaward. Everything as it happened was a slowed-down annoyance; they became waterlogged and clumsy, almost comical, as mishap piled upon mishap. Even Luke and Roman, the Asmat guides, were restless in the sudden motorless quiet of the waves. They seemed unreal to Stephen, like two figures from a silent movie, their facial expressions exaggerated, their request for permission to swim to shore uttered in a different universe.

Stephen was far away, in his head, writing everything as it happened. He was finishing the letter to his father, writing in his journal, picking out details to put down later: the taste of the salty, heavy sea, the gray air, the sight of the two Asmat men diving into the tawny waves and swimming away from the swamped catamaran, the sun moving ever lower in the tropical sky, descending into the swollen clouds. The waves were rougher now; a canvas duffel bag full of notes and film came untied and floated around the left canoe. And still Stephen Hesse was wandering through the letter to his father, trying to explain the odd, inevitable feeling that had taken hold of him.

At dusk, another wave hit and the tied-together canoes turned over. Their luggage floated away and then slowly, regretfully, sank into the Arafura. Stephen and Van Gropius clambered up out of the water, slipping and grabbing the slick wood backs of the upside-down catamaran. The two men said almost nothing to each other, following physical movement only with physical movement, fighting the sea. They reached under water and broke off pieces of wood from the catamaran's wall and tried to paddle, but the current was too strong. They gave up and straddled the upside-down canoes.

It rained all night, the low clouds dripping, covering them in a soft, salty mist as they drifted south and west, toward open ocean. A half-moon glowed. The two men were quiet through the night, awake, wet and cold, listening to the small rain on the waves, the canoes slapping the water.

At dawn the shore was a wavering brown line on a distant horizon.

"I think I can make it," Hesse said.

"Don't," Van Gropius said, shaking his head. "Stay with me. Just wait."

Van Gropius's dark hair was wet and flat against his skull; his mustache hung down over his upper lip. He looked sorry and frightened, heavy, like a walrus. He glanced away from Stephen at the empty Arafura. "There are boats coming still, you know. We *will* get picked up."

"I think I can make it," the young American said. "You don't know the swimmer I am."

He smiled over Van Gropius's head at the day starting to break, at the pink sky. He took off his pants and shoes, peeled off his cold, wet shirt, his singlet and underwear. He emptied their two petrol tins, spilling the now-useless chemical into the sea-water. He tied the empty containers to his waist with his belt, as floats.

"Well," he said. "I go."

AND THEN HE WAS IN THE ARAFURA, SWIMMING AND SWIMMING. He had stopped writing the letter. Now he was only the motion of his arms and legs, the warm, fishy-tasting water. A fragment of a poem fluttered through him.

> *In Freiburg station, waiting for a train,*
> *I saw a Bishop with Puce gloves go by.*

He swam straight and strong, and felt his heart pumping. A school of pilot fish light as a cloud of butterflies swarmed him, brushed against his face and arms, his thighs. He felt the rain start up, splashing him through the waves. An image of Maine beset him: walking down to the water through the trees behind the house, the wind nudging the branches of an old birch. Squinting into the northern sunlight. Lobster boats on the bay, the hum of a motor on the water, the gulls calling, screeching, complaining, as he picked through seaweed-covered rocks at low tide, his red tin bucket in hand, gathering mussels for his mother. Plopping the barnacle-covered creatures into his bucket of cool seawater, watching baby starfish drift in the shallow tide.

A gray nurse shark, aggressive, dumb, brushed up against Stephen's belly, jolting him from memory. She swam away slowly, uninterested. The waves had become gradually, rhythmically rougher, harder to get through. At that moment an awful coldness rushed through him, like death. He had a vision of himself, absurdly small, headstrong, flailing through an infinite ocean. The effort of swimming, the fear, the night with Van Gropius wet and cold in the Arafura, released an ache of loneliness inside him. He could feel it in his blood, making him cold. He could feel it in the seawater.

He realized then just how much he missed Sheila, how he carried it with him. He had a flash of her: green-gold eyes, skin that tasted like sunlight. Ah, Sheila, he thought. Sheila, my sweetheart.

The two petrol tins bobbing from his waist were a drag, were only weight now. He untied his belt and watched them float away. He opened his mouth and salty rain dripped onto his tongue. He felt better without the tins. He looked through the hazy morning at the mangrove trees lining the shore in the distance. The only thing was to keep moving, to keep swimming. He cleared everything from his mind except the feel of the sea on his body, the taste of it in his mouth, the ceaseless rain, the slight warmth of the early sun, the motion of his arms and legs cutting through the choppy, coastal waves.

Van Gropius could no longer see him.

# 2

## THE STARRY NIGHT

S TEPHEN HESSE AND HIS MOTHER LIVED AT 1062 PARK AVENUE during the school year, and in the summers they traveled up to Maine. They followed Stephen's father, Nicholas Hesse, and his new family, shadowing him and his second wife, their brood of fair-haired children and servants, as they migrated north up the Atlantic coast in the warm weather and then south again when the blueberry fields on Mount Desert Island turned violent fire-colors: brilliant orange, red, maroon, yellow. In the six years after Nicholas Hesse remarried, Stephen went from being the only child of a man worth more than $270 million to being the oldest of five children who would one day share that amount.

When their marriage broke apart in 1939, a phalanx of Hesse lawyers gave Nicholas's first wife the following: their son, Stephen, the immense apartment at 1062 Park Avenue, a cut-stone sun-filled cottage in the Hesse compound on Mount

Desert and money. Marguerite would live off the interest of a fortune that Stephen would come into on his majority. After that, if she hadn't remarried, she would receive an equivalent allowance from the Hesse family trust. The lawyers took care of Marguerite; no matter what, she would live out her life on a rich woman's income, although she had no wealth of her own and the baby, Stephen, owned the apartment in New York and the cottage in Maine.

NICHOLAS HESSE FELL IN LOVE WITH STEPHEN'S MOTHER when he was studying in England. Marguerite O'Keefe was the daughter of the woman who cleaned his rooms at Cambridge. The charwoman's daughter. Black curls framing eyes of the darkest brown. She was a short, plump woman, with wide hips and a full mouth, who read serious books. When Nicholas first met her, she only wanted to talk about T. S. Eliot.

Marguerite brought tomato-and-cheddar sandwiches on thick slices of black bread and a bottle of red wine wrapped in newspaper and read aloud Rupert Brooke's poetry while Nicholas punted the two of them along the river Cam, the sunlight green, the warm air full of the muddy river through a slow, English summer day.

> These I have loved: white
> plates and cups, clean gleaming,
> ringed with blue lines;
> and feathery, fairy dust.

The deep, musky smell of her, the soft hair in her armpits, her menstrual blood on his fingertips, seeped into him. Nicholas sat in his room reading Pater and Nietzsche, and his mind floated through her. Marguerite was silent, her intent brown eyes full of life, the stillness of her manner hiding the rush, the beating warmth of her. It was as though he were only his animal self with Marguerite, responding without willing it to the smell of her, to her full pink-lipstick-covered lips. Yes, she was a fortune hunter. She and her mother were a team. They had set their net wide for him, quiet, homesick American that he was. Nicholas was handsome in his way, fine blond hair already thinning, serious green eyes smiling above a square face and a muscular German peasant's body beneath his clothes.

And everything his father thundered at him in endless cables, and then in person in London, Nicholas knew the first moment he saw Marguerite standing outside Peter House in her sky blue jumper, her white stockings, the matching blue beret pulled down over her black curls.

In the earliest days of their romance he had sat at his desk while her mother cleaned his rooms. Mrs. O'Keefe swept, dragged a rag across the windowpanes, stripped the bed linen, emptied his rubbish bin of fingernail parings and crumpled-up papers. Marguerite *was* a fortune hunter. He saw her so clearly, and himself, too, falling into her like Alice down the rabbit hole. But, weirdly, it made him want her more; for the first and only time in his life he stood opposed to his father. He saw all of Marguerite as though he *were* her, as though he wore her skin.

They got married in the Registry Office in London and sailed back to New York. His father had pressured him relentlessly to come home, fretting in endless cables about Chamberlain; about the war that loomed over England; about his son, with his German last name, so far from home.

WHEN NICHOLAS FINALLY LEFT MARGUERITE, HE FELT LIKE A MAN surfacing from the bottom of the ocean. When they divorced, Stephen was still a baby, not even two years old. Dark like his mother, with her same impossibly pure velvet brown eyes full of loneliness, full of feeling. Nicholas couldn't be married to Marguerite: he shouldn't have married Marguerite. But he had. She was too foreign; she didn't even seem English to Nicholas's parents or their friends. No one knew what to make of Nicholas's marriage to a servant's child—the whole thing was as strange and scandalous as if he had married an Italian peasant while on holiday in Rome.

Marguerite was always quiet, sitting silent through tea parties in her honor, taciturn through formal dinners. No. He was to be king and she could not be queen. But he had held on to his first marriage until the last moment, knowing that he would have to push her away, but lost in her smell, in the warmth between her legs.

And in the end, Nicholas Hesse couldn't move far from his first wife and son: he bought another apartment in 1062 Park Avenue, in the opposite tower, which used a separate elevator. Even if he couldn't see her, he wanted her and the baby close by.

Less than a year after his divorce, Nicholas married Kiki Theale, a woman he should have been married to from the beginning. A blond and tall woman, a Texas lawyer's daughter, clever, light of heart, a golfer. Nicholas wanted to have Stephen with him and Kiki on the weekends, but when his lawyers brought up the idea to Marguerite, she exploded in a primitive rage. She would, she told them, kill her baby before she'd let that woman near it.

IN THE MORNING, THE DOORMEN AT 1062 PARK AVENUE WATCHED as first one and then the second Hesse wife strode across the black marble lobby. One blond and thin, full of movement, always pregnant, bulging with life, almost dancing, her long legs striding rhythmically, a fluffy mink hat framing her narrow, pretty face. It was as though she were drinking her life; her beauty, her wealth. It was her moment.

And the other, the first wife, slow, alone, or with her quiet, serious son, her wide, dark eyes absorbing every movement, every shadow, her pale skin, her black curls, turning gray, pulled back from her grave, un-made-up face in a knot. Like an owl, cruising past them, staring, blinking, full of contained violence.

"Good morning, Mrs. Hesse," the doormen murmured as she nodded and walked out of the heavy brass-inlaid doors, clutching her son's hand, ducking into their waiting car.

Stephen absorbed his mother's unhappiness, her mannerisms, her stilled anger, until they were so alike that they were a comic sight to the doormen at 1062. As far as they could see, the boy had nothing of his father about him. He had inherited his mother's Black Irish coloring, her thick-boned frame and heavy, fleshy legs. Unconsciously, the child mimicked her awkward, inward-turning gait, and the doormen smiled as the two dark heads bobbed through the gray stone canyon of Park Avenue, the boy carrying her shopping, mother and son so much alike that Stephen seemed part of her, not his own separate being. Other women tried not to stare as the two of them sipped their sugary tea and nibbled lemon cakes at Henri Bendel on Saturday afternoons, four dark eyes glancing up from pink porcelain cups with one anxious expression.

"That's Nicholas Hesse's first wife, don't you know," they whispered, and the hissing *s*'s of "Nicholas Hesse" saturated the heavy perfume and burned-coffee smell of the department store's dining room.

For Marguerite Hesse the only hours she was alive were when she was with this boy; lying on the beige broadloom carpet of his room, pushing tin fire trucks around wood-block towers, the nanny as distant as a cloud floating across the sky.

She got such pleasure from the child's physical presence: he was so bonny, his face surrounded by soft, loose black curls, his mouth and cheeks plump and babyish. It was an overwhelming, almost erotic pleasure to pull him to her and breathe him in, the smell of his hair and skin, the touch of his small hands, his childish voice in her ears. When she went out alone, he waited for her to return like a sentry at the gate. The nanny told Marguerite that Stephen sat, leaning against the front door, eating his lunch only if she brought it to him there. Marguerite could hear her son moving, breathing, on the other side of the door as soon as she got out of the elevator and put her key in the lock.

"Mummy," he would cry, his dark eyes lit up with her. "Mummeee," full of desperate emotion as though she had been gone a year, not an afternoon.

And as she smelled his hair, smelled his hot breath and felt how he trembled, her blood rushed with love for him. Even after he grew up and became cold to her, she'd remember these greetings—sitting in his wide room full of the unfiltered sun, sipping tea while he played with fire trucks and painted watercolor rainbows, kissing chocolate cake from his mouth—as the moments of happiness in her life.

BY THE TIME HE WAS TEN, STEPHEN HAD TAUGHT HIMSELF THE Greek alphabet and he could sound out the long-voweled opening of *The Iliad*. At school, at lunchtime, he sat in the library reading the lives of the Tudor kings and queens, and about the War of the Roses, laboriously copying the opening of *The Iliad* in the front of his notebooks, Μῆνιν ἄειδε θεὰ Πηληϊάδεω Ἀχιλῆος, as though it were a charm.

But up in Maine, he read Arthur Ransome and Kipling and kept a sketchbook that he wrote bits of his favorite poems in— *Here we go in a flung festoon, Half-way up to the jealous moon!*—and, with his colored pencils, drew the lobster claws and dead crabs he found on the beach. He sketched the sailboats anchored in the bay and his mother making blackberry jam; in her blue apron, black curls tied back in a kerchief, the dented aluminum pot filled with crushed seedy purple goo, the empty, boiled, sterile Ball jars all in a row.

Stephen loved to walk from his mother's summer house, with his sketchbook and pencils, through the blueberry fields and tangled hedges of wild roses that led down to the beach, and sit on a warm rock and breathe in the hot air and the sea smell and watch the sun glint white on the Atlantic. He would stay there through the afternoon, drawing or writing or leaning back on his elbows surveying the coast of Sutton Island and Little Cranberry.

THE AUGUST THAT STEPHEN TURNED ELEVEN, HIS MOTHER AN-nounced that he would stay with his father and Kiki for the rest of the summer season: she was going alone, back to 1062 and

then to England. Her mother was dying. Flushed with adrenaline at the thought of meeting and living with his father, Stephen
wondered at Marguerite as she roamed around the house, packing and weepy. She hadn't told him any of this—she'd kept it a
secret until now. Had she spoken to his father? Had she gone up
to Kiki's house while he was asleep? For the first time he could
remember, his mother was a mystery to him.

And so Stephen moved, wide-eyed, to his father's cabin, up
the road, around a cove, from his mother's—into a house that he
had never set foot in. Kiki gave him a bedroom at the top of the
house, painted white, with a round window facing the ocean, a
wicker table, a worn, soft patchwork quilt that covered the bed
and faded yellow muslin curtains that blew in the breeze.

His father wasn't there yet. He was still in the city, working.
Stephen felt like a peach slit out of its skin without his mother;
alone and bereft, sore and raw, unprotected from every sound
and smell, the light and cold and the all-of-a-sudden-strange
landscape that spread outside his new window.

His father's house throbbed with the unfamiliar noise of a
family: baby Vicky's wails before sunrise, followed by the muffled steps and soothing murmurs of her nanny; her brothers
shouting on the lawn before breakfast, down at the dock, diving,
splashing into the freezing Atlantic with hoots and hollers. His
half-siblings were blond and sunburned, scab-kneed and long-
limbed, like Kiki. They played and played, thundering inside for
lunch and then back out into the Maine day, and all the while
Stephen flitted like a ghost through the sun-drenched house.

His father finally arrived from the city with his secretary.
Trucks came and went, bringing meat deliveries, the mail,
boxes of corn and blueberries and tomatoes and bottles of milk,

rubber-banded lobsters and bushels of mussels. The servants cleaned and cooked; the rich smell of larded piecrusts and roasting beef seeped through the floors, into every corner of the house. The radio flipped on and off; the phone jangled, and all the while Nicholas Hesse was everywhere, his cigarette smoke, his deep, low-pitched voice, the hum of his existence vibrating through the warm days, like the wind shaking the pine trees.

Stephen stayed holed up in his room at the top of the house, filled to bursting with desire for his father. He felt how earthbound he was, how awkward, short and dark, pale and slow-moving among the sunrays who flickered across the lawn, out along the dock, paddling the waves in their red-painted cedar canoe. He read Simenon and Sherlock Holmes and started to plow his way, uncomprehending, through a Loeb edition of *The Gallic Wars* that he had found in his father's study: *Gallia est omnis divisa in partes tres.*

ALTHOUGH HE HID, LURKING, SHY, READING IN HIS ROOM, STEPHEN watched his father incessantly. He watched his sun-lined face wrinkle into a smile, he watched him smoke, he watched his thick fingers drum the table, watched how he ate, how he peeled an orange after dinner. He spied on him playing tennis with Kiki; he listened to him on the phone. He knew where Nicholas Hesse was as he moved around his house, when he moved his bowels. Stephen sat on the back stairs every afternoon listening to his father talk to the cook about the menu for the next day.

Father and son were formal, but a current of awareness flowed between them whenever they were around each other, at dinner, after lunch, when Nicholas would reach out absently to touch the boy.

His whole growing up, Stephen had kept his father out of himself. He had consciously held him away—but now he let the man's physical presence enter his soul: like an octopus squirting ink into its tank, those weeks in August Stephen's entire being was clouded with his father.

And unlike his half brothers and sisters, who had never known life without it, Stephen's confusion over his father in the deepest, most primitive part of his soul began. Because Nicholas Hesse owned the material world, it seemed that he *was* the material world. And that he had inherited the world from his own father, and before him his father's father, the Titan, Rudolph Hesse himself, blurred the distinction even further.

Nicholas Hesse owned the mines that scraped coal and anthracite, copper and nickel, out of the belly of western Canada; the pumps that drew oil from the black hearts of Pennsylvania and Texas; the forests that covered New York State, that lined the highways that ran up the Hudson River into Connecticut. He owned hotels; he owned museums and railways that ran from Albany into Ontario. Even in their childish, half-knowing souls, Hesse's children sensed the latent enormity of the wealth that surrounded him, as immense and unfathomable as the ocean. Their father was the source of life, of oil: the blood of America. Loving him was like loving the sun or the wind.

STEPHEN DREW AND WROTE INCESSANTLY, FILLING THREE NOTE-books in the two weeks his mother was gone, as if by recording what surrounded him he would be protected from it. He stayed in his room sketching the mist rising from the ocean at dawn, reading and reading, watching the rain drip-drop down his window. But there was a day that August up on Mount Desert, late in the season, when the sun shone so brilliantly that the sky and the sea melted together and the breeze fluttering across the waves through the birch and the ancient pine trees was so beguiling that Stephen could not stay inside. He ran down from his room, across the lawn to the overgrown path that smelled of hot earth and blooming roses. *Clunk clunk clunk* down the wooden steps that led to Hesse Beach, and then he was on the rocky shore breathing in the salt air, with the full morning sun glaring in his eyes.

The tide was out. The sea floor was revealed like a woman with her skirt pulled up; Stephen breathed in the rich, briny smell of sun-drying kelp, watched tiny crabs crawling among the barnacle- and seaweed-covered rocks. He walked up the beach, around the cove, into the blue, cloudless day, into the salty wind, watching how the Atlantic spread out to the horizon, a red-sailed clipper drifting in the distance, black and green islands floating across the bay, lobster boats humming, chugging out to check their traps.

He was dizzy with the sun, and for a while he walked along the rocky wall of twisted roots that bounded the beach, in the small shade of overhanging jack pines. He wanted to feel the water then, and he walked out to meet the incoming tide and let his canvas tennis shoes get soaked. How strongly it smelled of rotting crabs and sun-warmed seaweed, of seawater and the wind! After an hour he stopped at a private, sheltered point far from Hesse Beach: flat black rocks between skinny, gnarled pines, wild-sweet-pea vines crawling along the ground.

Stephen stripped off his clothes and lay on the rocks, arms and legs splayed out, absorbing the fat, white heat of the sun, the salt air blowing over him. He shut his eyes. The waves lapped

quietly; a gull called, swooping down; the tide came in, slow and
aggressive under cover of the bright, slowed-down day. Stephen
waded into the bay, naked except for his tennis shoes, and dove
into the shallow water. The sea was cold and thick. He swam out
until he could see around the cove to Hesse Beach, where his
half brothers were playing, diving from the dock.

When he left the little point, it was cool; the sun was setting.
Stephen was covered in scratches and mosquito bites, burned
pink, his hair stiff from the saltwater. The dock was deserted,
and as he climbed up the wood stairs, he could hear the family.
He emerged from the path on the lawn among his half brothers
and sisters, who were playing quietly, subdued, already dressed
for dinner, bathed, their hair combed. And there was his father,
in a gray seersucker suit and red bow tie, smoking, sitting on the
porch next to Kiki. Stephen flushed under his sunburn. He felt
how dirty and rumpled and wild he looked, like a shipwreck
crawling up from the shore. He felt his father's smile, his glance
from the back of the porch, like the evening sun glowing, illumi-
nating him.

"Ah, it's our explorer." Nicholas Hesse smiled and took a sip
of his drink. "Come, young man, and tell us what M'sieur Cham-
plain missed."

They all lit up around him, Nicholas Hesse's children, his
second wife; even baby Vicky became curious and toddled over
to him away from her nanny, her wide blue eyes taking him in. It
was as if they'd never seen him before, and they stared, looking
for a sign of who he was.

"Would you like a lemonade?" his stepmother asked.

Kiki Hesse was beautiful that evening, her blond hair
bleached from the sun, her lovely skin freckled, golden, healthy.

Delicate green peridot drops swung from her ears and a matching necklace twinkled around her neck. A white linen dress
draped over her long legs, her softly curved pregnant belly. She
was like a cat, assessing him, almost hostile. He could feel his
own mother hovering, staring at Kiki and his father through his
eyes.

"I think I'm gonna get dressed for dinner," he mumbled, and
ran inside.

THAT NIGHT STEPHEN READ LATE. HE OPENED HIS WINDOW FOR
the breeze and glanced out at the luminescent surf. His father
knocked on his door at one o'clock in the morning.

"Stephen," Nicholas Hesse said. "Let's go look for shooting
stars."

Then he was with his father, alone, walking through the
darkened, sleeping house, their soft footsteps echoing into the
quiet rooms. They went out the back, through the kitchen door,
up the gravel road, into an uncut field of Queen Anne's lace and
wild grass, climbing the hill, moving away from the ocean. They
were two noiseless rabbits, awake while the world slept, moving
through a hot night that smelled of the earth and Queen Anne's
lace, salt spray on the dry western wind. And the stars, millions
of yellow lights above them! Stephen's chest filled up to bursting
at how many there were, twinkling, bright, stretching on and on
to infinity.

He breathed in the night and the smell of his father, tobacco
and sweat, alcohol.

"There," Nicholas Hesse said, and pointed up. "Can you see
Polaris?"

He picked out blue Vega for his son, orange Arcturus, Alpha

Centauri, Andromeda and Perseus. His father stood still, smoking, looking up.

"You know," he said, "we really need a decent telescope up here. We'll have to get one for next summer."

Stephen thought he would float into the warm wind. He thought there was no other world than this dark and lit-up night, the earth stretching wide and warm, down to the ocean, opening itself to the star-filled sky.

# 3

## DEAD CHRIST AND THE ANGELS

I N STEPHEN HESSE'S SENIOR YEAR AT THE BROMLEY SCHOOL, HIS father was elected governor of New York State. But New York State was a million miles away from the northwest corner of Connecticut, from the boarding school in the foothills of the Berkshires, with its wide lacrosse fields that sat surrounded by low mountains covered in regrowth hemlock and spruce, that looked north to Massachusetts and south, down on the fertile ridge of the Connecticut River valley. The school's low redbrick buildings were on either side of Route 356: a chapel, the head-master's house, the dormitories and commons, which filled up with clanging steam heat and the smell of yeasty baking bread in the cold weather.

Stephen skied across the fields in the winter, half running, half sliding over the ice-crusted snow, breathing in the wood-smoke on the frozen air, stopping to sip hot, sweet coffee from his thermos, rubbing handfuls of snow on his red cheeks. He had discovered the pleasure of his body at Bromley. He wore his black, curly hair cut short and was almost squat, with a thick-boned, muscular frame and a powerful heart that let him motor his way uphill on his skis and run for the cross-country team. He loved running most of all. He won races for Bromley against Groton; against Saint Paul's. He played football and lettered in lacrosse. Even sitting in the library or at dinner, he seemed full of restrained motion, fidgeting, as though he would leap out of his chair at any minute.

It was also at Bromley that he started to feel the power of who he was in the world, the power of being Nicholas Hesse's son. Everyone at the school—the other boys, the teachers, even the headmaster and the chaplain—was aware when he was around, as though he glowed. He couldn't help it; it was a subtle but powerful rush, everyone silently agreeing that somehow he was out of the ordinary; somehow superior.

THERE WERE GIRLS, TOO—PARTIES IN THE CITY, ON MOUNT DESERT in the summer, dances at Bromley for the girls from McMaster and Miss Lang's. But although Stephen desired these girls and wanted to touch and smell them, he never had a yearning for any one particular girl or an interest in how or what they thought, in what they felt about him; that, he knew, was how his friends felt about their girlfriends. He vaguely associated his lack of feeling with his money, with his own lack of a father; and after all, he didn't care. The worlds of poetry, of photography, the blood rush of running cross-country races, were so much realer.

Stephen wasn't cold: he loved his friends with surges of emotion bursting into fury or pleasure with them. He jumped

into his friendships with the intensity of a man falling in love
with a woman. He followed his friends around Bromley, took
classes he wasn't interested in to be near them, read what they
read and then drew them into endless arguments, his mind racing as fast as his body could.

Yet there was never anything physical between Stephen and
his friends. All of that was weeded out in drinking too much, in
bruises from lacrosse, in the pain of long-distance runs up and
down the hills of northwest Connecticut.

AT THE START OF STEPHEN'S SENIOR YEAR, CHRISTOPHER MACNEICE
came to Bromley to teach Latin and the Euripides seminar.
MacNeice was hardly older than his students; he had only just
graduated from Oberlin College the year before. He had red-
dish-blond hair, a neatly trimmed mustache, and wore round,
wire-rimmed glasses over watery blue eyes. He was a small-
boned man, thin, strangely appealing, who would lapse into
long silences during class when he sat absorbed in a line of
ancient Greek as if he had forgotten the students around him.
He expected them to translate as rapidly and cleanly as he did;
they read *Helen*, *The Bacchae* and some choral fragments by
Thanksgiving.

The seminar met on the ground floor of Phelps House: two
long, lead-glass windows looking out at the painted-yellow
porch, at Route 356, at an old overgrown apple orchard beyond
it. The class met in the morning, and sunshine and the smell of
falling-apart books and stale tobacco smoke filled the room.

Stephen watched the young teacher in his thick-knit
sweaters and wool pants, clunky leather hiking boots. He loved
how MacNeice taught Euripides, cracking open lines like chest-

nuts. MacNeice showed them how complete ideas, entire com-
plexes of feelings, could be communicated in a scanned line of
six words. There was a slowed-down, hypnotic pace to his teaching, as if he were drawing his five students into his mind, enveloping them in the stop-start rhythm of translation, pulling
them inside the rigid, ancient language. To translate ancient
Greek, MacNeice said, you had to inhabit the mind-set of the
Greeks, with their obsessive gradations of time.

It was not only that there were five subtly different types of
past time to reckon with, but the Greeks had caught the endless
permutations of potential time in a net like butterflies and
pinned them down. Things that might happen or might have
happened, or probably would have happened or could happen,
for one's own benefit swirled around Stephen's mind. MacNeice
pushed them really to know it all—the only way to grasp at the
infinite beauty of Euripides was through the verbs.

Slowly, Stephen became conscious of a connection between
him and MacNeice; they were watching each other. All through
the fall, all through the early winter, he felt himself drawn
toward his teacher. During class, Stephen examined his teacher's
fingers as they turned the thin, black-inked pages of the Heine-
mann Euripides; the strawberry-blond stubble that grew around
his mouth and over his cheeks on the days he didn't shave. He
became almost giddy around MacNeice, flushed with pleasure;
provocative.

MacNeice assigned the first hundred lines of *Medea* over
Christmas break. Stephen started translating the play on the
train to New York. The verse was exquisite; each word in exactly
its right place.

*How I wish the ship Argo had never reached*
*Colchis, gliding through the blue Symplegades; No,*
*nor had the fir-trees been chopped*
*down to make its oars.*

It was snowing in New York when he arrived, not the heavy snow that northwestern Connecticut was covered in but soft, city snowflakes that melted on the sidewalk. The apartment at 1062 was warm and still. His mother had strung up garlands of pine along the hallway and a small tree sat in the library, decorated with hammered-tin ornaments.

As they always did when he returned from boarding school, they greeted each other and then retreated into their own rooms. Stephen sketched, worked on *Medea,* fiddled around with a short story he'd started up at school. Mother and son conjured the silence of a library in the apartment—quiet but alive. That was how they were comfortable now, both of them occupied with books and ideas and able to avoid the fact that Stephen was not happy to be home, that he didn't like being alone with Marguerite.

On Christmas, Marguerite cooked a duck with a prune dressing. Nicholas called to see if Stephen would come to the governor's Christmas Day cocktail party. There were people he'd like him to meet. But, no, Stephen wouldn't go over. Last Christmas when he'd emerged from his room in a jacket and tie to go to his father's party, his mother had collapsed in a terrifying puddle of tears on the floor in the hallway. Would he betray her on Christmas Day? Would he betray her after the two of them had bumped into Kiki that very afternoon, swaddled in mink, triumphant and smug, as she stepped out of a taxi holding shopping bags stuffed with gifts?

Stephen had stayed home with his mother last year, waiting for his father to call and find out where he was. But Nicholas never called, and as they spoke on the phone that year, it was clear that Stephen wouldn't come to the cocktail party.

"But we'll see you before you go back to school?" Nicholas asked.

Stephen could hear his half brothers laughing and shouting in the background. He could see Kiki and her brood, jolly with Christmas and Santa, mounds of wrapped gifts, the twinkling, massive tree, as clearly as if he were spying on them through a crack in the wall.

"I'll stop by before I leave," Stephen said, but again, they knew he wouldn't.

Couldn't his father just once come to Marguerite's? Just one time? Would they live out eternity in the same building using different entrances?

After dinner, in the library, Stephen and his mother drank champagne and had a *bûche de Noël* decorated with tiny meringue mushrooms. Marguerite had made up a tradition of giving Stephen a cashmere sweater from Brooks Brothers every year. This Christmas she handed him the box, wrapped in silver paper, watching while he lifted the top to discover a navy blue cashmere sweater folded in tissue paper. He reached down to touch it. The sweater was so soft and delicate it seemed peculiar, like an animal. He hadn't worn the one from last year, and now he would have two stashed in the back of his closet at Bromley.

"Thank you, Mother." Stephen smiled.

Marguerite was frowning, looking at her lap. "Don't you like it?"

"I do, of course I do." Stephen took the sweater from the box and pulled it over his head, pushed his hands and arms through the too-soft wool. He smiled at her.

"Oh, it suits you," his mother said, smiling at last. "That color flatters you. It always has, you know."

"Does it? It's wonderfully soft."

After Marguerite went to bed, Stephen stayed in the library watching the fire burn into embers. He was mesmerized by the flames, by the wood glowing orange. He was too upset to read. He felt like he was always pulling away from his mother, always sorry, always guilty. Her demand on him was too much, he thought. It was as though she forced him to be like his father, abandoning her over and over and over and over. He built up the fire, took off his sweater and dropped it into the flames. He sat there and watched as the cashmere burned in the fireplace, slowly turning into gray ash.

Stephen spent the next few days working on his Greek assignment, flipping through his old Jack London books. He finished his short story and then threw it away. Bromley reopened the dorms on the second of January, and Stephen was up there on the third, a full week before the term began.

FINALLY, CLASSES STARTED AND THE ROUTINE OF SCHOOL RE-sumed. New York slipped back into the remote world inside himself where it lived most of the time. Stephen became light-hearted. He felt like the frozen earth under the snow, full of life, waiting for the warmth of the coming sun.

ONE MUDDY APRIL MORNING AFTER CHAPEL, STEPHEN WATCHED MacNeice walk across the lacrosse fields, toward the path that looped west up from Bromley and into the Lakeville woods. His teacher was wearing a woolen cap, boots, a blue-felt pea coat. If he hesitated for a moment, MacNeice would vanish into the woods. Stephen wanted to see him. He couldn't control the urge to follow. Without thinking, still dressed for chapel in his suit jacket and tie and loafers, Stephen ran after him.

"Hey." He smiled, out of breath, catching MacNeice at the head of the path. "Want company?"

They walked together without speaking through the cold day, along the narrow passage that was veined with roots and rocks, surrounded by leafless elms and thin-trunked birch. Mac-Neice began rambling after a while; about the woods in Minnesota where he grew up; about how different in its soul, in its buildings and landscapes, the East Coast was from the midwestern part of the country.

They went two miles, to the summit of Parker's Hill, where they saw the Berkshires spread out below them, brown and green, and a lake in the near distance, gray in the hazy afternoon. They decided to walk to the lake.

"I like to walk, you know, really walk, like this for hours and hours while I'm writing. I think if I had my way I'd only ever be a tramp, just walking until I dropped asleep. Up the next morning, walking again."

"Writing?" Stephen asked.

"I'm working on a novel," MacNeice said, and smiled out at the view.

"Oh," Stephen said, weirdly deflated. "Really."

"Well, that's why I decided to teach this year. It gives me some time, some freedom to write."

All of a sudden the young teacher was standing in a different light. Somehow the idea of MacNeice as a writer, as a striving novelist, made him seem a little foolish. Stephen felt intuitively that his teacher wouldn't be a good writer, that his novels would be plotless, intellectual abstractions.

MacNeice looked at Stephen as if he would say something, and then changed his mind.

"So," he said. "Have you started the Huns yet?"

"The Huns?"

"Nietzsche, Schopenhauer, Goethe?"

Stephen shook his head, awkward, embarrassed at Mac-Neice's attempts. He wanted to leave; in that moment he only wanted to be alone. Out of the classroom, under the sky, looking out at the mountains, his teacher seemed an entirely different person, a prattling, self-conscious little man, intrusive.

"They call you heartless, but you have a heart, and I love you for being ashamed to show it," MacNeice said. "You are ashamed of your flood, while others are ashamed of their ebb. And that," he said, "is a little Nietzsche for you."

Stephen glanced at his teacher. He looked silly with his hat pulled low on his forehead, his glasses steamed up. He was smiling. Again Stephen felt the pull of the man.

"Shall we get going?" MacNeice asked.

They walked and walked, down from Parker's Hill into the woods. Eventually, the path widened into a deserted logging road. It began to rain, cold hard spring rain that still tasted of snow. Everything was mud and rain and nubby little buds poking out of naked wet tree branches. Stephen's loafers were soaked

through. His jacket and shirt were sopping. He took off his tie
and stuffed it into his pocket. Pools of rainwater had formed
along the ground and floated with twigs and leaves. An ancient
pin oak had fallen across the road and lay there, its bark orange
and rotting, melting away in meaty splinters from the downpour.
Then the road disappeared altogether under chest-high grass.

Finally, they emerged from the overgrown grass. It was like
stumbling upon Sleeping Beauty's house. Through the pounding
rain, an old-fashioned deserted summer cottage sagged, out of
breath, ready to collapse. Weeds sprouted up, through gaps in
the rotting porch, from under the stepless stairs. Glass windows
opened into a fathomless interior. The orange-brick chimney
alone stood solid, cheery, erect in the midst of the green-green
blur of the day.

Beyond the old house, down a sloping, overgrown lawn, lay
the wide lake they had seen from Parker's Hill. Mist covered the
mountains in the distance. The air was full of the wet smell of
the earth and the lake and the sound of raindrops falling on the
lake, *plash, plash, plash.*

The two of them walked down the lawn to a falling-apart
boat shed and ducked inside so MacNeice could smoke a cigarette.

The boat shed's walls had rotted open, allowing in stripes of
rainy daylight. As their eyes adjusted, old splintered oars, a
petrol tin, a rusted spade, emerged. A few moisture-swollen,
dirt-encrusted magazines littered the ground. MacNeice stood
smoking, looking out at the rain on the lake. They could see
trout rising up to the water's surface, opening and closing their
mouths over the raindrops.

MacNeice reached over to Stephen and pulled him close,

kissing him, there in the cold, dusty boathouse, his warm wet mouth full of tobacco. His nearness, his body, aroused Stephen. MacNeice opened his mouth and even in the half-light Stephen could see his small teeth, his pink tongue, and he felt weirdly alone—as if his teacher had left and only his body, his senses, his arousal, were there. Stephen covered himself in the smell and warmth of his teacher while the rain drip-dropped on his head and back. He dove into MacNeice until his teacher was the only world around him, and then he fell beyond him, floating, lost.

As soon as the rain stopped, a mass of twittering barn swallows flew out from under the eaves of the old house. The swallows flew in a gray arc of a cloud, swooping down over the boat shed, out across the water, diving, racing, gliding along the still, silver glass surface of the hidden Connecticut lake.


THE FIRST WEEKEND IN MAY, THEY DROVE DOWN TO NEW YORK City in Stephen's Karmen Ghia. MacNeice wanted to go to the Met. They wandered through the massive museum, spending hours in front of red-figure Attic vases and the Egyptian mummies. They sat on a bench opposite the strangely lit up darkness of the Dutch camera obscura and then went back, lost in the never-ending patterns of gods, snakes, scarabs and animal-headed goddesses, to gaze on the Egyptian sarcophagi.

For lunch they bought hot dogs and sat on the Metropolitan's wide steps, the May sun in their eyes.

"I'm tired," Stephen said, leaning back on the steps.

The day was familiar, like a part of himself. Every spring he had spent growing up in New York was with him as he looked out at the sun, at the taxis floating past, at the uniformed schoolchildren lined up.

"Let's go back in for just a bit," MacNeice said. "I want to see the Corots and the Manets."

Stephen followed MacNeice. He was heavy and bored. He felt the anger that was swirling through his soul, blurring his mind, become hard and focused. He thought his teacher was making a point—that he was the adult, Stephen was the child, the student. And Stephen felt like a child, like a sullen, sour child, following MacNeice through the echoing halls.

Finally, the two of them stood enveloped in the museum's marble floors and fluorescent glow and ceaseless patter of footsteps in front of Manet's massive painting *The Dead Christ and the Angels*. Stephen had never seen it before. He was surprised by it. The canvas was so big, and Christ seemed even larger than the painting, luminous, glowing silver-white like a close-up moon— so physical, more physical and present than the museumgoers strolling past them. And the angels—weirdly real, with their ugly, muscular bird wings, their sad faces. Stephen was nervous. His chest tightened and then he was full of the strange violence and anger of the painting. He knew MacNeice was looking at him, smiling.

"For behold," his teacher said, "the kingdom of God is within."

But the painting put Stephen in a worse, dangerous, mood. It had stirred him up. He became even quieter, angrier. Again MacNeice seemed to him petty, grasping. He had planned for them to go to Chinatown with some of his friends from Oberlin. Stephen wondered at his motives—did he want to show him off to his buddies, like a pet? *Look at me, I've got the governor's son along for chop suey.* Stephen refused to go.

"Come on," MacNeice prodded, smiling. "Watercress, mussels, jasmine tea."

Stephen couldn't. All of it seemed morbid, the museum a tomb, the streets and cars and buildings haunted, full of the humming of a million machines and car engines. He hated the city right then. As they stood arguing, he hated MacNeice. He hated him looking so piteous, hated his undisguised feeling, his delicate intellectualism. Blue eyes stared back at him from behind glasses, searching. There was something childish about MacNeice, vulnerable, like a young boy. Stephen knew he was still attracted to the man. But right then he only wanted to push him away.

"Well," MacNeice said, nodding his head. "All right. *Ave atque vale,* Stephen."

MacNeice walked down the enormous marble steps of the Metropolitan Museum, turned right and after a few moments disappeared into the crowd of upper Fifth Avenue tourists and matrons, nannies pushing baby carriages into Central Park.

Stephen drove as fast as he could out of the city, north along the Hudson River. The trees were bursting with life along the West Side Highway; brilliant yellow forsythia woven among the oak and willow. He opened the windows and the early evening rushed in; the warm spring smell of the earth, of the trees and hidden flowers and cut grass. He drove ever faster into the night, up into the cooler air of the Berkshire Mountains. He knew he was in the grip of something inside himself that he could not control. It was only the speed of the car rushing through the night that soothed him.

# 4

## *TRISTES TROPIQUES*

STEPHEN HESSE WAS UNHAPPY AT COLLEGE; HE'D SPENT HIS first two and a half years in Cambridge plunged into his work, trying to fill himself with English poetry, ancient Greek philosophy and art history, but he was only ever half occupied. A part of him was always unsettled, self-conscious among the other students, uncomfortable on the enormous, impersonal campus, in the dorms.

He joined the Fly, but he rarely went. The guys at the club journeyed in a different world, through a landscape of pretty girlfriends and married parents, cocktail parties, sailing trips with cousins, skiing together out west over winter break and a sureness about who they were and who they weren't. But they were friendly at the Fly and gentle, almost deferential, with him: his father, his uncle, his grandfather were former members. The men at his club were not surprised or intimidated by famous last names, by the sons of wealth and power. But even so, Stephen was self-conscious there, too.

College wasn't what he'd expected. But then, he asked himself, what *had* he expected?

He spent his weekends rowing on the Charles River, swimming at the pool, running endless miles around the gymnasium track, but the release from all his physical activity was only temporary; by Sunday night he would fill up again with the heavy, blood-born gloom that stayed with him all week.

Stephen began to feel that the university was a box over his being, filtering out the world. Words, the ideas in poems, no longer held him as they used to. He wanted to *do* something. For most of his sophomore year at Harvard he'd toyed with the idea of dropping out and joining the army. Nor had he met a single person at Harvard who caught his attention; he was only interested in his old friends from Bromley.

However, unexpectedly in the second half of his junior year, Stephen found himself engrossed in a class, bewitched by its professor, Laird Adams, and his anthropology class on ritual male violence.

Adams was a celebrity on campus, handsome and young and a brilliant lecturer. On some days he looked as tricked-out as Errol Flynn in an old-fashioned movie. But his ideas were futuristic. For Adams anthropology was not a genteel, Victorian science of sorting carefully collected data, documenting and constructing theories of exotic cultures. Adams's anthropology was vital—the only way to map his own society, to understand not only humanity in the Atomic Age but his own place in it. He was ahead of his time, and the Harvard undergraduates who clamored to get into his classes knew it.

That semester his course was, as they always were, oversub-
scribed. Auditors crowded the aisles of a lecture hall at the Museum of Comparative Zoology, cramped, notebooks balanced on
their knees. Stephen sat in the back, breathing in the building's
pleasantly stale smelling air, doodling in his notebook. The first
day of class, the first time Stephen had ever seen Professor
Adams, he strode into the lecture hall, shuffled his papers at the
podium, mumbled to a graduate student in the front row, set his
watch and then grinned up at his students as though he were
Hercule Poirot about to solve a whodunit.

"The art of war is of vital importance to the state," Adams
boomed, still smiling. "*The art. Of war. Is of vital importance to
the state.* And it has been since the first human animals emerged
in Africa."

Adams captivated Stephen Hesse. He followed the professor on an extravagant journey through time, across the world,
unfolding ideas to reveal patterns that led back across oceans,
spiraled out into past time and then trotted back up to the present.

Adams conjured images of warriors as he lectured: recount-
ing the histories of ancient Greek soldiers—outnumbered, dust-
covered, sweating, bleeding—battling Xerxes' Persian army at
divine Salamis; of fifteen thousand of Augustus Caesar's elite
Roman soldiers trapped, massacred, their living bodies nailed to
tree trunks by wild, screaming Germans in the Teutoburg Forest; Cortés fighting the Aztec cannibal-warriors, brilliant in ham-
mered gold jewelry, terrifying as they wielded their axes at the
conquistadores under the Mexican sun. The deep gutters of
World War I, full of teenage boys shooting at each other across
thirty yards of muddy earth.

Stephen felt as though he were running after Adams, catching glimpses of the world, of humanity, as a swirling, interconnected pattern.

There was no way to understand the behavior of man if you didn't understand war. Professor Adams lectured that it all started with the unit of father and family, what the Romans called the *paterfamilias:* the Father, who had absolute power over his children and their mothers, who could deny or grant life, who would, in different places and different times, transform himself into God, emperor, tribal chief, pharaoh, raja, king, or even the state—it was from the *paterfamilias,* in whichever mask he wore, that order, unity, and male identity emerged.

Stephen felt as if he'd been sitting in a dark room for twenty years and Adams was pulling back the curtains, letting the sunshine in so quickly and unexpectedly that Stephen was disoriented at first. But then, all of a sudden, he could see.

It was the first time he understood that his family existed within a rational, historical framework, that Nicholas was a sort of mini-king within a greater empire. His brain was going too fast. He wanted Professor Adams to stop for a moment so he could catch up with him.

Violence, Professor Adams told them, organized, ritualized male violence—not one creature spilling another's blood from greed or lust or hate, but sanctioned violence, with rules, parameters, penalties, uniforms and war paint, so that your fellow soldiers looked like you and you frightened your enemy with your strangeness—was how the *paterfamilias* bestowed identity. The Father's children, loyal to the death, fight his brother's children and two tribes are formed; two cultures develop and they exist and flourish because they are opposed and thus distinct.

Sometimes the professor showed reels of film in his class: flickering images from the late nineteenth century of tribal Indians from the Pacific Northwest in battle regalia, dancing a war dance, spliced into soundless color footage of American GIs driving Jeeps in Europe at the end of the last world war, to newsreels of Hitler's troops resplendent in their uniformity, goosestepping, saluting.

And always, at the end of every screening, the professor included the mushroom cloud exploding over Hiroshima.

"Robert Lewis, the copilot of the *Enola Gay*, wrote: *My God, what have we done?* in his flight log at the moment the bomb dropped," Professor Adams told the rows of bright, wet eyes drinking him in. "And what *have* we done? How can we understand the atom bomb within the anthropological framework of culture? How does it change our notions of ritualized male violence?" he asked. "Well, I for one believe we will find answers in the primitive cultures that remain on earth—before, that is, the few remaining ones disappear forever. We must study them as though our lives depend on it. Perhaps they do, no?"

Adams taught his students Lévi-Strauss and Malinowski, and Margaret Mead's and Sir James Frazer's writings, as though they were magical texts that revealed the mysteries of humanity. And Stephen read them like that, rooting around for the answers about his own life that he knew must exist inside them.

AT THE END OF THE SEMESTER, ADAMS TOLD THE CLASS ABOUT HIS upcoming project. He was putting a team together to go to Netherlands New Guinea, a rugged Dutch territory that lay a few hundred miles north of Australia. His aim was to be there for a whole year and conduct as thorough a study and documentation of the tribe as he could. Most of the people in the tribe had never seen a white man, Professor Adams said, had no idea of the world that existed beyond their valley. Stephen tried to imagine his professor's journey. He'd love to see a place like that before he died.

"So when people ask me why I think anthropology is the most modern of the social sciences, why real go-out-into-the-field-and-get-dirty anthropology is so important," Adams said, leaning over the podium. He was intimate in the enormous lecture hall. How did he do it? "Well, I tell them it's because, as Leon Trotsky said—you may not be interested in war, but war is interested in you."

THE IDEA OF PROFESSOR ADAMS'S FIELD TRIP HAD TAKEN ROOT inside of Stephen and it grew, nudging itself into his conscious mind. He wanted, he decided, no, he was dying to go with the team from Harvard to New Guinea. It didn't occur to him that his desire to go to New Guinea, his fascination with anthropology, was a result of Nicholas Hesse's lifelong passion for primitive art. The connection to his father was right in front of him, but he didn't see it. His fascination with primitive society seemed entirely his own.

Stephen introduced himself to Professor Adams at an end-of-the-year anthropology department cocktail party. He was the only undergraduate at the festivities, and he was invited solely because Governor Hesse had earmarked his annual gift to Harvard for the department.

"I'd like to go with you to the field. To New Guinea," Stephen said.

"Well, isn't that something," Adams replied, looking at him, smiling. He was contained and formal away from his podium. "However, you see, the trip to New Guinea couldn't really accommodate undergraduates at the beginning. In fact, honestly, I don't even know when or if it will come off at all. There are so many obstacles. But I'm eternally hopeful," he said, and shrugged his shoulders. "I'll keep you in mind."

"Yes. Yes, please." Stephen nodded. "It'd be amazing. I'd do anything—cook, be chief bottle washer, anything at all."

Laird Adams laughed, but he was closed down to Hesse, almost prickly.

Much later, Stephen would remember that cocktail party and the look in his teacher's eyes. But he knew that even if he'd seen the older man's contempt for what it was, he still would have forced his way onto the expedition. He wanted to go and live inside that primitive, primeval world as much as he'd ever wanted anything.

After exams, Professor Adams remained reticent, elusive, vague with details about the expedition. Stephen wanted to prove himself to the professor, prove his stick-to-itiveness—his dedication to his newfound ardor for anthropology. He decided to stay in New York that summer, alone, at 1062 Park Avenue and work at the Hesse Museum.

He would immerse himself in his father's collection of folk art and artifacts from antique civilizations while his mother, his father and Kiki spent the season in Maine. He would not spend his summer watching the two wives, dark and fair, in their separate cottages dancing their eternal silent dance for Nicholas.

BY AUGUST THE WHOLE CITY WAS MUFFLED UNDER CLOUDS OF pollution, of dank, humid air that darkened the sky and trapped the heat. Stephen rode his bicycle every day from upper Park Avenue, south, to midtown, to the four-story brownstone Nicholas Hesse had bought to house his collection of South American, Asian and African art. The museum had only opened to the public last spring, announcing itself with a black-tie gala and a discreet bronze plaque on the front door that read HESSE MUSEUM FOR PRIMITIVE ART.

Stephen was helping catalog a collection of Colombian fetish dolls. He spent his days typing up notecards in the buzzing fluorescence of the windowless basement file room, padding around barefoot on the broadloom carpet and then bounding up the stairs, two at a time, to check with a curator, to examine the fragile fabric dolls, dressed in embroidered miniature *chalupas,* mute, tiny disintegrating things: cupped in his hands, they felt like they had no weight at all.

Through all of August he read *Tristes Tropiques;* at lunch and late into the night. But he read slowly, struggling with the French. Ten paragraphs were a day's translation. But the book's world, Lévi-Strauss's memories, engulfed Stephen; he too was on the foul, overcrowded steamer fleeing France from the advancing Nazis, chugging over the rough Atlantic to Martinique. He was in hot, magnificent Brazil watching as it was plucked of its indigenous people, its culture, its great natural beauty, like a chicken being cleaned for dinner. He had never read a book like it before; its sentences, its images, haunted him, rolling through his mind, through his dreams, in waves.

STEPHEN LEFT THE MUSEUM LATE IN THE AFTERNOON. HE LIKED to ride his bike, exploring the humid, half-empty city as it came alive at dusk with people leaving work, comparing it, in his mind, to Lévi-Strauss's descriptions of Calcutta. He rode up through the park, through the filth and heat of the dying day, and then down Lexington Avenue as the East Side of New York sank from wealth to filth. How quickly it happened! In a block the whole world changed; nannies pushing carriages turned into armies of secretaries, of tired faces above black-and-white maid's uniforms, clerks rushing for the subway.

The bus exhaust and grit grime of midtown became garlic and cumin, onions frying in lard, as he traveled farther south, farther east, passing unwashed storefronts, their doors flung open and box fans churning desperately in the thick air. Down on the Lower East Side, the sidewalks were full of people: children and teenagers in front of burst-open fire hydrants, laughing and splashing, glancing up as Stephen flew past on his bicycle.

On Friday afternoons he took the ferry out to Fire Island. Stephen loved the old boats that plowed through the muggy haze over Long Island. He went every weekend to visit Billy Chadwick, a Bromley friend. Billy was tall and blond, his pink skin so fair that it was almost translucent, now burned red and freckled from the summer sun. He had a largish nose, long thin arms and legs and intense, close-set blue eyes. He always had a slight smile on his face, a Mona Lisa smile, Stephen thought, but with a nasty tinge.

Chadwick, sober, had a softly ironic demeanor, but when he was drunk, when the two of them were drunk, they were holy terrors. They roamed Fire Island at night, getting into fistfights with each other, flying off the boardwalks into clumps of poison ivy, harassing anyone they happened to run into. Every weekend they built an enormous, menacing bonfire on the beach and Billy brought out his father's old shotgun and fired up at the night sky, shooting at glass bottles or taking aim, he claimed, at the Russian rockets whizzing above them.

Billy's father was a banker; his mother, a self-taught painter. She painted houses, dogs and cats, and endless primitive portraits of Billy from old baby photographs; his face was always strangely distended in his mother's paintings; only his intense, close-set blue eyes made them recognizable representations of her son. The oil-on-canvas portraits were among Stephen and Billy's favorite things to throw into their bonfires to get them going.

The Chadwicks spent August in a rented house on Nantucket, leaving Billy to his own devices in their A-frame on Fire Island's bay side. It was a gloomy house, shaded by a copse of pine trees on one side and the neighbors' much larger house on the other. Billy was out there all week, and when Stephen arrived from the city with *The New York Times* and a few bottles of gin and a bag of groceries, they would sit on the Chadwicks' deck, which looked out over a swampy patch of poison ivy and sea grass, and drink and slap at the mosquitoes and sand flies.

Stephen woke up early at the beach, even after a night of drinking. He made coffee and rode Billy's bike around the boardwalks, past the sleeping houses, looking across the soft white dunes at the swell. He thought it was all so beautiful, the smell of the sea in the dawn mist, the sound of the boardwalk's planks *thump-thumping* under the bicycle tires.

One Saturday in the middle of that August, just after dawn, he saw another biker, far ahead of him, breezing through the thick, briny air. For no reason he sped up to catch her. It was a woman; he saw that even in the distance.

She turned to him when he was at her side. Green eyes flecked with gold and black stared at him. Intense. And as she smiled, they were full of humor.

"Morning," she said.

"Hey," Stephen smiled.

The two of them kept riding without speaking. She wore ragged khaki pants, a T-shirt splattered with paint, ripped-up canvas tennis shoes, and her hair was tied up under a red bandanna. Stacks of heavy silver bangles encircled her wrists. She rode up toward Watch Hill and the boardwalk emerged out of the trees and the landscape became the early, blushing sun, the ocean, the dunes covered in beach grass.

She introduced herself when the boardwalk ended and they got off their bikes.

"Hi," she said, smiling. "I'm Sheila Egan."

"Nice to meet you." He nodded. "I'm Stephen Hesse."

He watched his name register with her, surprise cross her face and then disappear.

"I'm walking up to the old lighthouse," she said. "Do you want to come with?"

He followed her and again they didn't speak. Sheila had beautiful, sun-browned golden skin. Her round, odd face appealed to him, although he knew his Bromley friends wouldn't call her pretty.

She was much older than he had thought at first; her girlishness was an illusion of distance. But as they stood there, facing the sun and the sea, and she turned toward him and then back to face the dry northern wind, her hair tied up in the colorful cloth, he decided that she was the most desirable woman he had ever encountered. Her hands, her arms, her teeth, her legs and ankles, were all perfectly formed. Her whole being was gold and full of the sun's warmth.

"I MET A GIRL," STEPHEN SAID WHEN HE GOT BACK.

"Sheila, right?" Billy said. "Oh boy. Well, that was bound to happen. She's local fauna."

"What d'ya mean, oh boy?"

"Oh, just that she's been out here forever, since I was wee. Her father's some bigwig advertising guy who hasn't been sighted for years. I think he gave her the place. Sheila lives out here year-round. Most of the year, anyway."

Stephen nodded, thinking.

After breakfast the two friends sat on the deck drinking gin and tonics, playing cribbage for a while and then backgammon. And all day long Stephen felt how Billy was uncomfortable, bottled up in spite of the alcohol. Finally, he looked at Hesse and drew in a big breath.

"Listen, Stephen. As old Patsy Chadwick would say, Sheila's not, er, um, well, she's not your type."

Stephen smiled, "Oh yeah? How's that?"

"I'm not saying that to get you excited, man."

Stephen smiled and took a sip of his drink.

"I feel responsible for you. I mean, you realize that, right, Stephen?"

"I do," Stephen said, and looked away from his friend at the gray wood boardwalk. "And you shouldn't. I don't need to be responsibled."

Early evening was settling over the island. Stephen smelled the smoke from someone else's barbecue. He was hungry.

"Shit, Hesse. She's old, she's got some freaky French boy-friend who comes and goes. I think she's totally broke. And on top of everything, she's truly weird."

"I just went on a *bike ride.*"

"Oh, take pity on us, Lord, for we know not what we do," Billy sighed.

"Give it a rest, Chadwick," Stephen said peevishly. "Are we ever going to eat anything?"

Although Stephen was up with the dawn the next morning biking around for almost three hours, he didn't see Sheila. It wasn't until the next weekend that he found her, on the other side of the island, sitting on her deck. Sheila's house was an old saltbox, built at the edge of a dune, with a large, weather-beaten wood-plank deck that looked out on the ocean. She had ringed the deck with rusted Savarin coffee cans full of overflowing sweet-pea vines, silver-leafed lavender and tall poppies, erect on strong stems, brilliant red with black chaps. She was sipping from a mug of coffee, watching a pine tree covered in hundreds of monarch butterflies.

"Shh," she whispered to him. "Look."

Stephen put the bike down and walked onto the deck. The tree's trunk shimmered, alive with iridescent orange and gold and brown. He stared at the creatures, at the black veins that ran through their velvety wings, which pumped slowly up and down, in time with the waves crashing on the beach.

"Why do they do that?" he asked her.

She shrugged her shoulders. "It's just the way they are, Stephen Hesse."

"Hey," he said. "I liked walking with you to the lighthouse last weekend."

She smiled up at him. "Do you want breakfast?"

THE OLD SALTBOX WAS DECEPTIVELY SMALL FROM THE OUTSIDE. As he walked in, the house seemed to expand, breathing light and air. The walls and floor were painted white. Faded printed fabrics, hung across the windows, threw filtered shadows, and everywhere was driftwood, junk she had found washed up; mobiles of hanging beach glass and shells, tin cans planted with herbs: chamomile, thyme, dill weed, mint, coriander. The house was seductive with the sea, with its smells and the wind that blew up from the beach. Sheila's hair was down that day and he saw how dark gold it was, the color of her skin.

She cooked him thick, smoky-tasting bacon, pancakes full of bananas and soft walnuts, chicory coffee sweet and rich with canned milk. Stephen looked at three stretched canvases leaning against the wall, covered in bright splashes of colors with black paint dripped over them.

"Are those your paintings?"

"They are."

"Oh," he said, looking at the canvases more carefully. "I like them."

"They're not for sale," she said, smiling an odd, indecipherable smile.

"Okay," he said, taken aback, aware that somehow he had stumbled into the wrong place.

"Okay," she echoed.

After breakfast Sheila took off her shirt and stood in the kitchen in a white bra and her shorts.

"I can't do the dishes in my shirt," she told him. "It always gets soaked. I don't really believe in clothes that much at the beach."

Stephen sat on one of her worn cotton couches with his cup of coffee, smiling. She looked amazing to him, sun-brown, hairless. She was silent as she washed up. Did she know he was staring at her? Did she know how aroused she was making him? The only sound in the house was from her silver bangles clinking together as she worked.

Stephen watched Sheila move through her magical little saltbox house, her arms still soapy, her lithe, nut-brown legs full of strength, and he recognized something about her, her manner, her loneliness. Somehow she reminded him of himself. Sheila put on a phonograph while they were eating breakfast, and Dave Brubeck's piano filled the house; Stephen had the urge to dance. He thought he was going to start laughing out loud.

He stood up and unbuttoned his shirt. Sheila turned and stared at him.

"Why are you taking your shirt off?" she smiled. "Are you making a pass at me?"

"I think I am," he said. "Is that all right?" He was elated, full of the light and the waves and the pleasure of the day.

"No." She shook her head, still smiling. "No, it's not all right. I have a boyfriend. A steady."

Stephen didn't know what to say. She was still smiling, encouraging. He felt her body, her spirit, open up to him.

"Oh. I'm sorry then."

"Are you?" she laughed. "You don't look a bit sorry."

"Well, I'm not sorry if you don't want me to be."

"I know that. No, no, I like you, Stephen. I'm only teasing. Why don't you stay for a while? Jean's still in France for another few weeks and I'm going batty out here all by myself. It's gotten so bad that I'm contemplating a return to the West Village."

"Is that where you live in the city?"

"It is. On West Eleventh."

Sheila opened the glass doors to the deck and pointed at a wicker chair.

"I'll be right back," she said.

Stephen was confused, excited—he had no idea what she meant for him to do. He lay back on the chair and gazed up at the sky. Sheila came back out in an orange-and-black bikini and lay down on the deck to bathe in the morning sun. Stephen stayed on his chair, willing his body to be still, waiting for her to say something, to make a movement, all the while breathing in the smell of her coconut oil and listening to the crash-lull of the nearby ocean hitting the beach.

After a while he realized that Sheila had fallen asleep, and he got up. He felt weird to be that close to her, so aroused, when she wasn't really there. He wanted to bend down and kiss her, breathe in her smell, but he was afraid she would wake up. Instead, he smiled at her sleeping face and rode back to Billy's, in love with the seawater and the pine trees, the soft ocean wind and the boardwalk.


STEPHEN CAME OUT TO FIRE ISLAND ON THE EARLY-MORNING ferry that Wednesday without telling Chadwick. He brought bags of groceries, delicacies for Sheila (wine and gin, chocolates, smoked trout, bread and delicious English Stilton, salami, tins of raspberry jam and a bottle of Ribena syrup), who met him at the dock with her baby buggy to shuttle the bags up to her place. For himself, he brought his sketchbook diary, his pastels and colored pencils, *Tristes Tropiques* and his battered pocket Larousse.

He drew her that afternoon, after lunch, sketching with charcoal, drawing her as she lay on the deck, but he was frustrated; he couldn't really get her. He tried jotting down descriptions of her, of the impossible, incongruous outfits that looked so good on her, the liquid motion of her limbs as she walked along the beach.

She told him that she had turned thirty that spring. She was nine years older than him. He imagined her as a little girl, Lewis Carroll's Alice Liddell, wandering, daydreaming in a pretty blue cotton dress on the day he was born. She told him her mother was part Iroquois, "and so was Winston Churchill," she declared, and he wrote that down, too. He took photographs of her with his camera. At least, he thought, when he was back in the city he could try to draw her from these photos.

They drank steadily but not heavily all day, drawing, reading, sleeping, running down to the beach and swimming in the rough, cold open sea and then in the late afternoon sat down with tall, lime-filled gin and tonics. The high with Sheila was so different than the loud, carousing violence and physical emotion that erupted from him and Chadwick during their drunken nights. The slow, continuous ingestion of gin and sunshine, the ocean breeze, nibbles of cheese and mortadella, pickled gherkins, thick slices of dark pumpernickel, gave Stephen a sweet, contemplative drunkenness—which was exactly the point, Sheila explained. Liquor, in the right amounts, was the key to a jail cell. The perfect mix released your soul from its prison, and as it flooded into your being, you became, she said, exactly who you were meant to be.

He thought of asking her about her boyfriend, Jean. But, really, he didn't want to know, so he only looked at her and said nothing.

Stephen felt that he had never eaten before Sheila fed him. She laughed as she cooked, and chattered and hummed along with the records that she played all day. She poached flounder in white wine, baked the tomatoes that grew on her deck, stuffed peppers for him with raisins and onions and sweet, nutty, dark wild rice; but most of all, she loved lemons. Lemons, she said, were the proof of a divine being.

"That's one of the sadder things about Americans," Sheila told Stephen while they were eating dinner, grilled eggplant and a cucumber salad—spicy, lemony, full of mint, sprinkled with sugar—and drinking a bottle of the Haut Médoc he'd brought for her. "Especially *your* kind of Americans. Boy, do they not know how to eat. It's like they don't have mouths or tongues, just little funnels that they stuff with boiled lima beans and overcooked roasts."

"Oh, I see," Stephen said, laughing. "Aren't you an American? You sure talk like one."

"I don't know," Sheila said, and ran her fingers through her hair. "I don't know what I am."


AFTER DINNER STEPHEN GOT OUT *TRISTES TROPIQUES*, THE Larousse and a stubby pencil, and started translating.

"What's that?" Sheila asked. She was doing the dishes.

He flipped through the pages and translated a paragraph. She was so quiet that at first he thought her mind had drifted away from him.

"So," she said, shaking the suds off her hands into the sink, "what is *that* supposed to mean?"

"Well, Lévi-Strauss thinks that in America, nature's only been degraded—that there's nothing wild left—or truly old like in Europe—there's only new, dirty cities and polluted, humiliated wilderness."

"Well, what about Yellowstone, all the redwoods? Y'know, all that stuff out West?"

"I guess he'd say that isn't *real* untouched wilderness. I mean it's no longer the way it was before the Europeans got here, is the point—undiscovered, unmapped, the real wild. It's all a part of the Known, is Lévi-Strauss's point," Stephen said.

Sheila walked over to the couch and sat facing him. She nodded her head and lit a cigarette.

Sheila was a slow and avid reader. He had watched her spend half an hour reading and rereading the same few pages of a book, pencil in hand, jotting notes in the margin. She loved what she called "natural poetry": poetry that occurred without anyone meaning for it to be poetry. An idea, a phrase, a recipe. She didn't like this, he could tell.

"Have you ever read the Sermon on the Mount?" she asked. She was still in her bathing suit, and she sat smoking, her lovely brown legs open, her long, soft hair loose over her shoulders. Was she offering herself to him? He looked at her mouth, at her dark lips. He wanted so much to taste them.

"In church, I guess. Not recently." He smiled.

"You should," she said. "I don't think you'll find any other written thing more beautiful."

"No?"

He wanted to touch her so badly that he worried he might

inadvertently reach out and grab her. She stood up, engrossed in her thoughts.

The yellow glow from Stephen's reading lamp illuminated her smooth body in the moonless dark. She walked into the kitchen and made a gin and tonic for him, one for herself, and walked out onto the porch. Sheila stretched her arms wide, her silver bangles clinking on top of each other, her body opened up to the night. Stephen sat with *Tristes Tropiques* in his hands, looking at her strong back and muscular thighs, her beautiful arms. He had to touch her. He would try; he couldn't help it. He was all cramped up from holding back.

Stephen turned off the lamp and walked out onto the deck. Silently, he put his arms around Sheila. It was so dark that at first it was hard to distinguish the ocean from the air. He felt how her heart was beating and her skin was cool. She smelled of the fresh mint she had chopped for their dinner and her lavender soap and a faint musky smell from her armpits and her groin.

He ran his hands along her skin, feeling the goose bumps rise up under his fingertips. He cupped her breasts, feeling their weight under the soft nylon of her bikini top. She didn't pull away.

Stephen's eyes were adjusting to the dark. He could make out the trees, the boardwalk, the ocean swell, the rhythm of the waves, their soft, endless crash and withdrawal. He knelt in front of Sheila. The sand on the deck was gritty beneath his knees. He pulled down her bathing-suit bottom and she stepped out of it for him. She stood still and he unfolded her; he opened her up and tasted her. He felt like he was licking the sea, swallowing an oyster. He listened to the grunts and little moans in her throat, the sounds of a nursing baby. He was so aroused by her softness, by the taste of her. He wanted to crawl up inside of her.

A fawn emerged from the pines and walked up onto the deck. Its round black eyes regarded him, unsurprised, and then it was gone, its hooves clapping across the boardwalk, back into the pine forest. Stephen disappeared into Sheila, into her taste and the night; into the sea smell and the waves and the wind blowing across the island.

ON FRIDAY, STEPHEN WALKED TO CHADWICK'S. BILLY'S HOUSE seemed impossibly gloomy and dark after Sheila's. Chadwick himself was simmering, jealous that Stephen had spent so much time with Sheila. A neighbor had spotted Stephen sunbathing on the other side of the island.

"Suit yourself," Billy said to him. "But don't blame me when she starts asking for 'artist grants' or however she's gonna put it."

"Why so nasty, Chaddy?" Stephen asked, shaking his head, smiling.

Stephen's mind was swirling with ideas, with thoughts about women and men, about couples, about sex. He wanted to talk to Billy. He had never really thought about it before, what it meant to be in a couple, to belong to another person. He turned around the idea of marriage: a wedding, a ring.

He was intrigued by the idea of trying to melt two lives into one, like Aristotle's somersaulting beings. He wanted to possess Sheila. Would she possess him?

Billy was sour. He didn't want to talk about women or marriage. The subject bored him. He'd been alone, waiting for his friend, all day. Billy wanted to get drunk. So Stephen sat frustrated, in his head, while he and Billy drank themselves past their hurt and irritation.

Gradually, Stephen's mind slowed down, calmed by the alcohol. He looked at Billy. He loved him; he always had. Billy was his friend and he was happy to be there, with him. In a way, it was a relief to be away from Sheila. But he was covered in her pollen, and as he sat looking at his old friend, full of affection, Chadwick seemed far away.

STEPHEN WENT BACK TO THE CITY ON THE SUNDAY FERRY. AS THE week unfolded, he was less and less interested in being there, in his work at the museum, when he could be on Fire Island. He began to think about the fall, and he slowed way down. The idea of being away from Sheila for three whole months unsettled him. She was so elusive anyway.

At night, alone, in the endless rooms and hallways of his mother's quiet, hot apartment, he continued translating *Tristes Tropiques,* like a medieval monk poring over a manuscript.

He followed Lévi-Strauss through Colombia, into Bolivian gold rush country, traveling with him on a steamship, struggling for every meter as it sloshed through dense jungle rivers.

*Here what we consider as the traditional roles of the sky and the earth are reversed.* Stephen copied Lévi-Strauss's words into his notebook. *The sky is the region of shapes and volumes, while the earth retains a primeval softness.*

It hit him one morning as he woke up in his bedroom (still full of old toys and books, framed posters of King Babar and Queen Celeste, the collection of baked-clay Roman figurines that Nicholas had given him) why he had to go back to school: he would be an anthropologist, like Lévi-Strauss. Like Professor Adams. He would get himself on that expedition to Netherlands New Guinea.

Stephen wanted to know the last, disappearing stretches of

the wild. But *not* as a tourist. He wanted to go as a scientist: really study it and know it and feel it. All of a sudden a fully formed plan appeared in his mind, as though it had been growing inside of him all summer. He knew the way to get on his professor's field trip to New Guinea. He, Stephen, would fund the expedition himself; he knew Nicholas would approve. He would drive up to Mount Desert next week and discuss it with his father. The thought of it—going into the true unknown, what he would learn, who he would become—opened him. It was as though he'd been hiking and had stumbled across a view; he saw the immediate future for what it was, and saw that he could change it—not just experience it.

He was almost in a trance as he left for Fire Island to go to Sheila. He needed to see her; somehow, she was tangled up in this new idea, his need to travel to the other side of the world, his unexpected clarity.

He packed a knapsack and bought a liverwurst sandwich to eat on the ferry. The whole way out, his thoughts and plans bounced through him, dizzying him, rattling his nerves. But underneath all the noise in his mind he was still, like a trout hiding behind a rock at the bottom of a fast-rushing river. Really, he only wanted to see Sheila.

He walked from the ferry west through the island, toward her house. A current of cold air sharpened the breeze; the season was shifting. When he got to Sheila's house, it was shut up, the door locked, the windows covered over. He walked up onto the deck and knocked on her door, but there was no reply; he put his ear on the glass door, but it was silent. Still, he had an odd feeling that she was inside. He took off his pack and wandered around the saltbox, peering in through the windows, looking under the deck. No one was there. Just sand and poison ivy and the rumble of the close-by waves.

Why hadn't she called him in the city? He had given her the telephone number at both Marguerite's and the museum. He felt sick. Her boyfriend was back from France. And she hadn't even thought enough of him to get in touch, to say when they might see each other again.

Stephen walked away from the little house, down the board-walk. He could not face Chadwick. He went out over the dunes onto the empty beach while his excitement, his life, dripped out of him. His chest was aching; every breath made it worse.

He kept hoping, a dull waiting and hoping that she would come home and see him on the beach and walk out to get him. A white-tailed deer wandered down the dunes, nibbling at the beach grass. A speck of a battleship floated on the horizon. The water was muddy green close to shore, blue-black in the distance. The waves were rolling in, sideways rolling tubes that crashed into white foam, one after the other. A flock of seagulls gathered in the shallows, feeding.

As he sat on the beach, Stephen's rage at the world grew so intense that it was no longer a part of him; it was a blowtorch burning in his face. But after a couple of hours, his fury congealed in his blood as the cold, heavy self-loathing it always did. I am a child, he thought, and lay back on the sand. He would die there; he didn't care. But his mind was still hopeful, whispering for Sheila. If only he could have seen her.

The sun set and Stephen stood up. He walked down the boardwalk to catch the last ferry.

# 5

## THE SEARCH

ELEVEN HOURS AFTER STEPHEN HESSE DOVE INTO THE WARM, silty Arafura Sea and swam away from his swamped catamaran, a pink slip emerged from the Dutch embassy's code room in Washington, D.C. The Dutch ambassador telephoned Jane Lyle, Nicholas Hesse's personal secretary, and told her: Stephen and Erich Van Gropius were missing at sea.

Jane Lyle treated the Dutch ambassador's news as though it were an enormous political snafu—a runaway horse that needed to be reined in. Lyle, a delicate, middle-aged blonde with deep brown eyes, had worked for the president of the United States before Governor Hesse hired her. And it was in a crisis that who she really was, what she was really capable of, became clear: she telephoned and telegrammed, placed trunk calls and cables, pressured, cajoled and organized until, twelve hours later, her heart pumping with adrenaline and Dexamyl, she, Hesse and his bodyguard were at Idlewild, boarding a 707 for Los Angeles.

In Honolulu, after a meeting with Hesse, the governor of Hawaii and three different airline executives, Jane Lyle chartered a jet to fly them to Netherlands New Guinea. While they waited for their plane to be prepared, Hesse disappeared inside the Hilton, hiding from the newspapermen who padded soundlessly through Honolulu like so many hyenas sniffing after a carcass. Lyle went shopping. She bought sunglasses, disinfectant, mosquito nets, insect repellent, quinine pills, flashlights, batteries, chocolate bars and butterscotch drops, the most expensive pair of binoculars she could find and wide-brimmed canvas hats.

It was hot in Honolulu. Lyle was sweating, her olive green dress was dark under the armpits, down her back, her high-heeled pumps snapping at the cement sidewalk, up the hotel stairs, finally muffled on the carpeted hallways.

She'd brought dozens of red folders full of work from New York: correspondence, half-written proposals. When she tapped on Hesse's door, she found him surrounded by these papers, by the smell of gardenia and blossoming frangipani and the hot, wet air that floated in through the open-louvered windows. Lyle wrote telegrams to the Albany office, ordered Coca-Colas and tuna melts from room service and gave her boss a Dexamyl.

They sat there, the two of them, working quietly until the front desk rang to say that Mrs. Marguerite Hesse was on the line from New York City. Without speaking, Lyle got up and walked into the hallway, shutting the door behind her. She stood there waiting, watching the bellboys rush down the corridor, the hotel guests saunter past in their flip-flops and bathing suits, all the while listening to the low-pitched murmur of her boss's deep voice through the door. She only left when she heard Hesse bang down the phone and begin to weep.

Jane Lyle walked outside, behind the hotel, to the Honolulu Hilton's beautiful, small swimming pool, which was surrounded by empty beach chairs. The pool was lit up by underwater lamps, and refracting aqua light flickered into the Hawaiian dusk. Unthinking, she strolled down the stairs to the pool, seduced by the glowing water, by the impossibly sweet smell of jasmine and gardenia in the humid air.

She took off her sandals and sat at the pool's edge, first dipping her toes and then submerging her nylon-stocking-covered legs into the warm water. Wide white-and-yellow frangipani flowers had fallen into the pool and floated aimlessly. She, too, wanted to drop into the water and swim among the waxy petal blossoms, but instead, she leaned back and watched tropical night leak into the sky. In just a few moments she would go back to work.

ON THE CHARTERED JET OUT OF HONOLULU, NICHOLAS HESSE SAT in an empty row, gazing out the window at the plane's wing, gleaming in the colorless sky. A thick red folder sat on his lap, unopened. He was beset with images of Marguerite. He saw her in England, before the war, when he had first known her. In a way, Marguerite hadn't prepared him for other women; in a way, she wasn't like a woman. She lusted like a man, like he did, with her hands and mouth and tongue, with her nose, with her body. They had been violent together in his narrow, uncomfortable little bed in Cambridge; greedy, as though they would have eaten each other if they could have.

And Stephen. Stephen. He thought of his son then, just born, crawling on Marguerite's wide, low breasts like a blind newborn bat, dark and furry, piteous, reaching for her with his weirdly adult-looking long fingers, rooting with his tiny pink mouth for her nipples. She was so satisfied then, a Madonna and child. *Look what we've made,* Marguerite had said over and over, her dark eyes black, bottomless, as she smiled up at him still dopey from the gas. *Look what we've made.*

Nicholas could barely stand the thought that glinted in his soul now, sickeningly, the thought that somehow all of this— Stephen's trip to the Asmat, his interest in primitive art—was to please him, was tangled up with Marguerite and him. All of a sudden Jane Lyle was at his seat, interrupting his thoughts. She asked a question. How much she disliked him, his secretary. He felt it always, even now as she stood there smiling, her manicured hand (pink fingernails, a simple gold wedding band) on the armrest.

Mrs. Lyle was smarter than him; he admired her for it. She was beautiful, too, but she had no sex. She didn't really care about money, Mrs. Lyle, although she happily accepted his gifts, the bracelets and brooches from Van Cleef and Arpels, the Eastern Airlines stock. He knew she mourned her job with Eisenhower. He knew she still loved her former boss with a pure, blood-deep devotion and measured every man against him. Nicholas felt her dissatisfaction with him, with the work he did, every day. She was like a horse bred to carry a king into battle who had wound up saddled by a country squire.

*No,* he shook his head at Jane Lyle as she stood there peering at him with her question, with her checklist of important things. He wanted her to go away. And she did.

But he couldn't resist her for long. He beckoned her back, and they began to work. Or, rather, Jane Lyle composed letters for him to sign, suggested responses to inquiries and wrote cables to send to the States when they got to Hollandia, the capital of Netherlands New Guinea.

Nicholas could only drink Coca-Cola on the plane. His stomach was sour from the aspirin and Dexamyl he had been chewing, from the worry over Stephen that coursed through his head, a constant high-pitched whine; the drone of the jet engine. He fell into a light, half-awake Dexamyl sleep and dreamed of Hesse Chapel. He dreamed of the stained-glass windows his grandfather had had installed in the little stone church up in Haleyville. Aware that he was dreaming, Nicholas watched the stained-glass Jesus gazing into the beyond, his arms open, his white robe parted so that the whole chapel was covered in the red-golden glow from Christ's heart, in his pouring-out light-filled blood.

In this dream of his boyhood, on the jet flying to New Guinea, Nicholas saw his grandfather sitting in the chapel so clearly that it was as if he had flown back in time. There was Rudolph Hesse, sharp nose and thin lips, white hair combed back, running his fingers, unseeing, across the pages of his worn Bible and mumbling, *If you love those who love you, what credit is that to you?*

In Hollandia, the heat overwhelmed them. The sun was too close. Electric, disconnected thoughts buzzed through Nicholas's mind as he walked out of the plane into the wet heat, into the mud and jet-fuel smell. And the staring; it seemed like a thousand eyes were regarding him, blinking, watching with one single, fluid, all-encompassing stare.

The pressmen, the photographers, were waiting for Hesse, and as he walked down the stairs from the airplane, flashbulbs

exploded into the too-bright day like lightning on the sun. The
Dutch colonial administrator walked across the airfield. Under
the brim of his white cap shone two dark blue, intelligent eyes.
And Nicholas knew; right then he knew that Stephen was dead.
He'd known it in New York when Jane Lyle read him the am-
bassador's message. He thought he would vomit.

"Good news!" the administrator boomed in his Dutch-
accented English when he reached Hesse's side. "We've picked
up Erich Van Gropius, alive!"

THEY FLEW TOWARD THE SOUTHERN COAST, TO THE TOWN OF
Merauke, in a Dutch DC-3. Van Gropius was waiting for them in
the administrator's headquarters. But Hesse could barely look at
the young man. He wanted to smash him to pieces; he only heard
his voice, irritable, bouncing around the white-painted walls, re-
peating in English, *I take no responsibility! I told him, Don't go!
He is headstrong, the young Hesse, no? I could not stop him! I
said: Don't go, don't go! I take no responsibility for you!*

Nicholas had not really slept in three days, he thought, although he was no longer sure how to count time. The hours had
unraveled and tangled as they sank farther and farther down into
the Southern Hemisphere. And the desire for his son's body—to
touch his child, to feel his face, his skin, his soft black curls—was
growing in Hesse's brain like a tumor, nudging thought, vision,
rational understanding, toward oblivion. Jane Lyle buzzed
around him, murmuring familiar names in his ear, sending a
constant stream of telegrams back to the States. She smelled
sour in the New Guinea heat; her sweat was musky and strong,
the chemical scent of her dry-cleaned clothing emitted a vapor
that wafted after her.

He was aware of the movement, the roar of activity around him: the press, the Dutch military, the aircraft, the Australian Army's helicopters, New Guineans everywhere, the strange, vowel-click of their language penetrating through to his soul. He was a fish in a fishbowl surrounded by a distorted, surreal landscape. *I did this,* he thought, *I killed my son,* during a press conference that Jane Lyle had set up in the equatorial morning sunshine next to the airfield.

The newsmen jabbed and prodded, little boys poking at the goldfish in its bowl.

"Could ya tell us how much the search for Stephen's costin'?"

"Ya reckon yer son was eaten by the savages?"

The Australian press hated him the worst, or at least they were the most up-front about it. Every question was money, money, money. He was grotesque from his wealth, not really human to these men. Nicholas had always known, had been taught, that the world outside his family loathed him because of the money and that they always would, whether it was to his face or behind his back. Or else they clustered around him like street urchins swarming a European tourist in Calcutta, loving him no more than the beggar loves the man who throws him a few rupees.

The sun was too much; his eyes hurt.

"Ya reckon Stevie brought it on himself, waving all those tobacco sticks at the cannibals?"

"Hey, Governor Hesse, what kinda search ya reckon the Dutch would make for me if I fell off my motorboat?"

Sloth, anger, envy—*Bless those who curse you . . .* And if Nicholas had been born with nothing, like his grandfather, like Marguerite, what then? What would it be to walk among men as a man? He had spent his youth fantasizing about giving every penny away as soon as his father died—it was like a fantasy of leaping off a bridge. How seductive the idea of flight was, the release of being between this world and that, the release of throwing everything away. But he couldn't. He was afraid. In the deepest part of himself, he knew he wasn't distinct from his money; the Hesse millions were in his blood, like his father and his mother were in his blood. And he was who he was.

He saw Jane Lyle standing off to the side, watching, frowning as the press conference spun out of control. She would answer their questions if he would let her. She would tie these men into pretzels and leave them to bake under the tropical sun. Yet she couldn't answer their questions. She didn't understand, really, what was going on. How could she?

But she toiled for Hesse in New Guinea; for the rest of her life Jane Lyle would remember every day of the search for Stephen. In the heat and discomfort, bearing the deflected dislike of the Dutch brass. She worked ceaselessly from the little closet of an office they gave her in the colonial headquarters. She even set it up so that when she and Hesse went out on the Navy DC-3 he would be separate, protected from the press. She banned all cameras on Hesse's plane.

They were to fly along the coast, over the sea and then out to the spot, twenty miles offshore, where Van Gropius had been found a full day after he and Stephen went missing. The Dutch Navy had plucked him—only him—out of the sea, half-dead, clutching the overturned catamaran.

Lyle *was* sorry for Hesse. She, too, knew that his son was dead and knew, without being told, that Stephen was the child of Nicholas Hesse's heart. It all seemed to her, this search which was

more like a military operation than anything she had ever seen—
the Australian Army helicopters thudding through the daylight
hours, the dozens of Dutch Navy Seals who dove into the murky,
treacherous sea, the constant drone of Cessnas buzzing through
the air, the thousands of New Guineans and missionaries in
dugout canoes searching the mangrove swamps, probing every
inlet—it seemed like all of it was only the rage, the mourning of
a stricken god, stomping and thundering against Fate. Even she
couldn't stand it that they couldn't find the boy's body. It was like
torture to her to think where he might be.

Lyle clipped the papers as they came in. She filed everything. Perhaps, someday, Hesse would want them. On the day
they were to go out on the DC-3, Lyle clipped a piece from *The
Sydney Morning Herald* that she didn't save for her boss; instead, she sent it to her sister in San Diego.

THE KING OF AMERICA SEARCHES FOR HIS CROWN PRINCE, the
headline ran. It was written by a reporter who had followed an
American Catholic missionary, Father Michael Dougherty, and
some of his flock from a local village as they joined in the search
for Stephen Hesse, puttering out into the chop in their small,
rickety motorboat. Father Dougherty claimed that young Hesse
had stayed in their village on his way upriver only a week ago,
and that the two Asmat guides who were with Hesse when his
boat swamped were members of the priest's own flock.

When one of the converts wondered at the fuss the white
man was making, at the planes and boats and helicopters swarming the coast, at the hundreds of uniformed Dutch soldiers and
thousands of New Guineans out braving the rainy-season waves,
all for one missing young man, the missionary fell silent. Then
carefully, slowly, choosing his words delicately, he had explained

to his boatful of Asmat men that Jesus taught if you save one soul, you save the whole world. As the Asmat villagers stared at him, unspeaking, the missionary went on: "And this boy's family, well, it's like they are the headmen—the kings—of America. And America, well. America is the king of the world."

*And so you see,* Jane Lyle wrote to her sister in the newspaper's margin, *the kind of public relations we're up against here. More soon from Mosquitoville.*

THE DC-3 FLEW OVER ENDLESS MILES OF MUD AND SWAMPS, OVER scrubland and muddy clearings that held villages of a few huts, built up on stilts, with blue smoke seeping from their thatched roofs, rising up, like a prayer, into the gray sky. Narrow rivers and streams wound lazily through swamp and salt flats toward the tidal shore, and then they were out over the Arafura. Hesse and Lyle were up front; the press in back, out of sight, behind a shut door.

Nicholas Hesse sat holding his binoculars to his eyes, watching an enormous crocodile plow its way into the shallow sea. A few miles out, a group of gray nurse sharks were gathered, nose to center, feeding. The sea was the color of pencil lead. Stephen was a boy to him; a baby. How could he be out there alone in this endless ugly sea? Nicholas had a wild idea to jump out of the plane and fly, coasting along the waves, like a seagull, searching for his boy. He glanced up through the open cockpit doors at the pilots. And then he fell asleep.

In a few minutes the seawater was clear, a beautiful blue-green color. Jane Lyle could see the ocean's sandy floor and the slow-moving shadows of turtles and fat dugongs, the occasional metallic flash of a barracuda school. The plane banked left and headed back north toward the Asmat coast.

"Mrs. Lyle," the captain called to her. "We're just a few moments from where they found Erich Van Gropius. Shall you wake Governor Hesse?"

She looked over. Nicholas Hesse was in a deep sleep. The binoculars were resting on his chest, and his face was lit up by haze pouring in from the oval window. His hands were open at his sides, palms up, fingers outstretched, poised to reach out, to enfold his son in his arms.

"Let him sleep." She sighed, shaking her head. "Let him sleep."

# BOOK 2

---

*Alas, our frailty is the cause, not we;*

*For such as we are made of, such we be.*

—*TWELFTH NIGHT*

# 6

## ALL MEN ARE BROTHERS

THIS IS THE POINT THEN, IN LATE AUGUST, THAT STEPHEN had arrived at: he was back in the city from Fire Island without having found a sign of Sheila Egan. He was stumbling around New York, too upset to do anything that he meant to do and unable to get the vision of Sheila's empty beach house out of his head. He was about to start his senior year, and the possibility of Professor Adams's field trip to Netherlands New Guinea winked in the distance. But everything seemed flat and colorless to him.

He knew that Marguerite, who'd spent the summer in Maine, alone in the cottage, would be back in a few days. He was listless at 1062 Park Avenue, lying on his unmade bed, drinking ginger ale and eating ham-and-Swiss sandwiches from the deli on Lexington. He didn't think he could sit up, much less pack and drive to school. But he knew that if he was in the apartment when his mother walked in the door with her bags of dry tomes and jars of blackberry jam and quiet, accusatory loneliness, he would come undone.

It had become so difficult between them that Stephen never wanted to visit with his mother anymore; she caused a disruption in him, in his physical self, that took him weeks to recover from. He thought it was his pity for her and her fragile nervous state that stubbed his soul and released a dreary sadness into his being. But it wasn't pity or guilt that he felt.

Although he didn't know it, her presence—her face, the delicate, wrinkled skin of her neck, her short-bitten fingernails—stirred his ancient feelings for her: need and hurt and desperate love. All of it bubbled inside him, along with an inchoate sense of shame for her and himself. He felt stuck to her. He couldn't stand it that when they were alone together, they immediately became the same isolated, fatherless duo they had been his whole childhood. He understood now that she had kept him so close to her when he was young because she suffered from terrible loneliness. Nonetheless, he held it against her. He thought she had broken something inside him when he was little. It took everything Stephen had to look outward, grasping onto the belief that there was something more to him than who he was when he was with his mother.

The last few times Stephen had gone up to Mount Desert, they spent the weeks of his visit in silent, brutal battles. To avoid her anger, he slept. A surreal fatigue, as strong as a Demerol haze, set into his being as soon as he arrived in Northeast Harbor. When he woke and visited with his father for an afternoon sail to the Cranberry Islands or had dinner with him, Marguerite wouldn't talk to her son for days. She demanded his attention, his sympathy, his allegiance (there would never be a truce with Kiki), and he had refused her all three.

No. He didn't want to be in the apartment when Marguerite returned.

So away he went, driving fast, released for a few hours from his gloom and hurt by the pleasure of his car in motion as it sped north, up into New England.

CAMBRIDGE WAS STILL HOT WITH LATE SUMMER. STEPHEN WATCHED the school year start up around him, slowly at first, floods of new students rushing in, bringing the smell of the world with them. He avoided the commotion as much as he could. Finally, the day before classes began, he roused himself to call his father in Albany.

The governor thought the trip to New Guinea sounded marvelous. Of course Stephen must go, and of course they would offer to fund the expedition. He would put in a call to Professor Adams that day.

"How interesting!" Nicholas said. "What an opportunity it is for you, my boy."

In the 1930s, Nicholas himself, just out of Harvard, had gone off on his own adventuring, driving along the dusty, unpredictable roads of northern Mexico. He'd driven through the tiny, remote villages that had no electricity or running water but housed communities of folk artists and potters, who baked clay in earth ovens and painted pre-Columbian patterns on their ceramics. It was on that trip, all those years ago, that Governor Hesse's fascination with primitive art had started. His collection had begun with a trunkful of the magnificent Mexican pots and masks and bowls and hammered-tin paintings of demons and saints.

"What an inspired idea, Stephen," his father said, his deep voice rich with enthusiasm and approval.

Stephen was taken aback by the rush of pleasure flooding through him. He was standing at the end of his dorm hallway, holding the telephone next to his face and smiling, all of a sudden blushing.

"Yes, I think so too," he said.

Why should his father's enthusiasm make him so happy? It was the first time his mood had lifted since he'd encountered Sheila's locked-up house. The idea of his father fixing everything with Adams and the university elated him. Stephen had known that Nicholas would help, but still, the actuality of it stunned him. It was as though his father had bent his wing down so that Stephen could crawl up onto his back and fly with him.

DURING THE FIRST WEEK OF CLASSES, STEPHEN GOT A MESSAGE IN his mailbox to come by Professor Adams's office. Adams's office was spectacular. The floor was covered in beautiful Persian rugs. Sun shone through old lead-glass windows, lighting up the rich reds and greens in the rugs and the mahogany shelves, which were crammed with hundreds and hundreds of books. The professor's collection of Benin bronze figures stood along a shelf behind his desk, and antique lithographs of the native peoples Captain Cook had encountered hung on the walls. The office felt like a gentleman-explorer's lair, a place of warmth and comfort and reflection, but Professor Adams himself was cool and tight, sitting behind his desk.

"I'm very pleased," he said when Stephen sat down, "to offer you a place on the expedition to New Guinea."

"Oh, how amazing!" Stephen almost leapt up out of the chair.

The professor smiled and nodded. He started to tell Stephen details—when they would leave, what vaccinations he needed to get, the way they'd fly there, the equipment they had to bring, who the other team members were. Stephen wrote everything down in his notebook.

"Thank you so much for giving me this opportunity," Stephen said.

"No, Stephen. I think I should be thanking you."

Stephen didn't know what to say. He was embarrassed. Was it so bad to want to go on this expedition? But then, Nicholas wouldn't have agreed to fund the thing if it were wrong. The thought of his father reassured Stephen.

"I can't tell you how much I'm looking forward to the trip."

"Oh yes. I am as well. I think this is important work we're going to do, Stephen. I'm very glad to have you on board." The professor paused. "We've decided not to leave for the field until after graduation exercises."

They sat there smiling at each other in silence. Stephen realized that his professor was through with him. As he left the office, he looked back to say good-bye, but Adams was already back at work, engrossed in some typewritten papers he had spread out on his desk.

AFTER PROFESSOR ADAMS INVITED HIM TO COME TO NEW GUINEA, Stephen dove into library research, pushing Sheila to the back of his mind. He read everything he could find about New Guinea.

The country emerged from his books as a fantasyland, another world; most of the terrain was unmapped rainforest, mountains shrouded in clouds, lowland jungles, all of it full of birds of paradise and tribes of people living in the Stone Age.

Stephen hadn't imagined that a place so primal existed. Even in black-and-white photos, the country looked like Eden, seductive with mountains wrapped in clouds and swollen rivers that twisted across the flatlands. The thought of New Guinea made everything else seem like waiting.

But even as he immersed himself deeper in New Guinea and his classwork, Sheila was on his mind. He pushed her phantom away and she resurfaced in his dreams. He was miserable for her. He had her address in the city and began to write her notes, letters. Sometimes he sent her drawings. She didn't respond and he continued—the fantasy that no one was reading his letters made it easier for him to send them. Stephen wrote to her every day, documenting his life, his studies, describing the people he saw in the library, walking through Harvard Square; he wrote about his loneliness, his desire for her. Did she really mean to disappear from him forever? Why had she left Fire Island without a word to him? Was she married?

BY THE END OF OCTOBER, HIS YEARNING TO SEE SHEILA WAS UN-bearable. The more he wrote to her, the more he thought about her, the more demented he felt. On Halloween he drove down from Harvard and got two speeding tickets in Connecticut. But even so, he didn't slow down. He found her apartment building in the West Village before nightfall.

The neighborhood looked like a forgotten slum to him. Bits of garbage floated across the sidewalk; dour, boarded-up warehouses lined Washington Street; the sky was clouded over with brown pollution; even the smell of the river seemed heavy, full of oil and metal. He saw the men who worked down on the piers trudging up Charles Street, looking down, hands in their pockets, not talking to one another. It was so cold—the wind off the Hudson stung his face and his ears.

And then there she was in front of him, solemn, lovely, standing in the narrow, dark hallway of her apartment. Sheila didn't seem surprised to see him.

"You're quite a letter writer," she said.

Stephen blushed and shrugged his shoulders. He was ashamed of the letters now.

"No, really," she said. "I think they're incredible. I've saved them all for you."

"Oh."

She stayed there, standing in her hallway, looking at him curiously.

"Stephen, you know—remember? I have—well, had—a boyfriend. He's French and lives half the year in Paris, which is why maybe it seems to you that I'm alone. But I'm not really, you see."

He nodded. He didn't want to hear it. There she was.

"I've been with Jean for a very long time. He's in Europe now, and we've fought, as we had this summer when you and I . . . when we met at the beach, but—but you should know this happens a lot between me and Jean."

Stephen nodded again. He didn't care. She had fought with her boyfriend; she was here alone. The steam heat clanged in the pipes. Finally, he realized that she wasn't telling him to leave. She was talking, but he did not listen. She was so beautiful, he thought. She was wearing black pants and an old pink sweater, frayed and splattered with oil paint; her hair was back in a scarf. He had interrupted her working.

He walked over to her and carefully, delicately put his arms around her shoulders. He stayed like that so he didn't have to look at her face. He held her and breathed in her hair and her skin-smell and the turpentine and linseed oil on her clothes. He fought the urge to weep. Why, he wondered, was she the only person in the world who could stop this aching in his chest?

He spent the night, wanting her over and over, unsatisfied even when he was covered in her and she was sleeping so close to him that he felt her heart beating and had her taste in his mouth. He couldn't fall asleep. He looked at her apartment, which was illuminated by a streetlamp. She'd painted the walls white and the floor black, and her canvases were everywhere. The sounds of the night—footsteps on the hallway stairs, voices on the street, foghorns from the river, a truck rumbling over the cobblestones—kept him company while his mind worked away.

Stephen felt as though he'd been living alone in an obscure, remote place, somewhere faraway and hidden, that he thought was only his. Then he found Sheila there. But how could he feel that if she didn't? She aroused him in a way that he hadn't even known he could be aroused. It was as though she peeled his skin off, like the rind from an orange, so that he was no longer Stephen Hesse but his own essence, just the will and consciousness that existed in his mind and dreams. Surges of hot pleasure, wordless, greedy pleasure, pumped through his blood as he touched her and tasted her and then swelled up, filled to bursting with her.

When he was away from her, if he didn't control his mind,

life slowed down to minutes and her absence blew up and tortured him moment by moment.

WHEN SHEILA WOKE UP, STEPHEN WAS DRESSED, READY TO LEAVE,
sitting on the side of her bed looking at her.

"Would you like to go up to Vermont with me next weekend?" he asked.

She smiled, drowsy, nesting in her sheets and blankets and
pillows, a cat curled up in the sun.

"Sure," she said. "Maybe."

"It's incredibly lovely up there this time of year, right before
the snow falls."

"Yeah?" She was purring with sleepiness.

"I can arrange for us to stay in my uncle Toby's barn."

"A barn?"

"Yes," he laughed. "My uncle Toby, he's not really my
uncle—he's one of my father's cousins. Anyway, he collects
Americana. He has this amazing converted barn that's empty
most of the year. He's not there until Christmas. Do you want to
come with me?" But he said it like this: *d'yawannacomewimee.*

"All right." She smiled. "Why not? I mean, I think that's fine.
I need to be back by Tuesday by the very very latest, though."

"Oh. Oh, don't worry. I'll definitely have you back here by
then. No, you won't believe your eyes. It's amazing."

IT *WAS* AN EXTRAORDINARY PLACE, SHEILA THOUGHT. UP AT THE
top of a steep dirt road, past a falling-apart stone wall built before the Civil War, sat a wide painted-blue barn gazing out at an
amphitheater of mountains. From the car Sheila could see a
pond, covered with floating leaves, and a birch forest beyond. It

was cool when she and Stephen arrived—perfect and clear, windy and full of the mountains.

They had driven all day, spent the night at a roadside motel, got up early and drove through almost another whole day, but as she breathed in the cool afternoon sunshine, the fatigue left the bones in her back and legs. Sheila stood next to Stephen and glanced up at the barn and the mountains that rose in the distance.

The barn was immense. The old haylofts had been knocked out and the roof was raised three stories off the ground. Enormous glass doors and windows covered the side that looked out at the pond. It was like a cathedral, Sheila thought, walking inside: enormous, full of filtered light and an ashy old-smoke smell from the fireplace.

"I'm going to go chop some wood for us, for the stove, to keep us warm tonight," Stephen told her.

"Oh, right," she said. "Do I help?"

"No. You take it easy. Maybe find Toby's bar and make us some drinks."

"That I can do."

STEPHEN WAS NEVER STILL: HE WAS SWIRLING, LEAVING, COMING, going—full of impatience and ideas. She didn't really believe what he said to her, how in love he was, how he thought about her all the time. She saw his passion and how he had directed it at her, and she saw, too, how it overwhelmed him. He was full of feeling but it was tinged with something impersonal. It wasn't really about her, she thought. Or maybe she just didn't want it to be.

Why her? she wondered. There must be dozens—hundreds—

of suitable and even not-so-suitable girls lined up at Radcliffe or on Park Avenue for a chance at him. She shook her head, took off her coat and draped it on a chair.

Now that they were there, her misgivings about coming to Vermont were swelling. She did not understand Stephen Hesse. She didn't even really understand why she was there. Somehow, she hadn't been able to refuse him. It was as though he were a soldier on a one-night pass begging her to be with him before he was sent back to the front. What a thought! But it stayed in her head.

Sheila walked around the barn, gazing at the hundreds of record albums of jazz, opera and classical symphonies that Uncle Toby had lined up, alphabetized and stacked on thick painted-white shelves. She saw Stephen through the window, chopping wood in fluid strokes. He was strong, and when he slowed down, she thought, he had a beauty of movement: like a buck, full of contained speed and strength. He was unusual-looking and attractive; she had thought that when she first saw him riding around Fire Island on his bicycle. Right then the sight of him stirred her. It wasn't true that she felt nothing for him.

The barn was full of Americana: old dolls, antique maps of New England, a spinning wheel, advertisements for the *Maid of the Mist,* World War I posters, lovely, handworked quilts hanging on the walls, an old Union uniform from a Vermont battalion, pressed between glass sheets. High up on the wall over the dining room table hung an enormous, dirty canvas banner (also framed under glass) that read, in hand-painted red letters: ALL MEN ARE BROTHERS. Sheila smiled. Some more than others, she thought.

A musty-smelling pantry sat next to the mudroom. A black

telephone peeked out at her from a shelf, surrounded by cans of baked beans. Sheila picked up the receiver and listened for a dial tone; Uncle Toby was on a party line. She found a bottle of gin and poured herself and Stephen enamel cupfuls and walked outside, onto the flagstone porch. Stephen was standing, sweating, catching his breath over a pile of wood that he'd stacked into a neat triangle.

"Would you like a cup of gin?" she asked, smiling.

"Oh yeah. Yeah, thanks." He took the cup from her and sipped it, looking out into the distance.

"Hey, Sheila—I have to go inside and get the stove lit up and start dinner. But why don't you stay out here and enjoy the sunset?"

Again Stephen left. Why was he so afraid to be around her? She felt sorry for him. Light from the dying sun had spilled all over the mountains; pink clouds lay on top of the green forest. The gin tasted good, and she smoked a Pall Mall.

Sheila walked over to the pond to see the landscape from a different angle. How would one paint all of this without becoming sentimental? She could never paint the mountains as they were right then—frightening, magnificent, melancholy. Jean had told her to look at Cézanne for a month—stop painting and just look. It was what she felt about a landscape, a person, a building, a flower, that she had to get down on the canvas, he said, not just torture herself about being true to the essence of the object in front of her.

But Sheila knew all that and still she never felt she could get it onto the canvas. Here she was, back at the questions that always deflated her—did she have real talent? Or was she just able to recognize beauty? The clouds on the horizon turned from pink to red to violet. Her mind wandered, following a squirrel up the tree, the wind rustling through the grass, the leaves, the rippling surface of the pond.

As the sun set behind the Green Mountains, Sheila drifted through the corridors of her life, opening doors and seeing things and people and places she hadn't thought of in years. She had worked and worked since art school, preparing for the moment when she and her art would be yanked out of obscurity. She had been painting forever. Jean had hundreds of her canvases in his New York storage space. Nothing ever happened. There was the odd dealer or gallery that sniffed around her, but it never came to anything. Not one painting of hers had ever sold. And slowly—it was very slow (it had started before she met Stephen at the beach)—the horrible knowledge that she would not have a career as a painter was emerging into her consciousness. No, she couldn't stand it. The idea made her want to pull her hair out.

She didn't want to be an "artistic" woman. She didn't really want money—she had enough from her father to live. She'd always thought that riches would come when her paintings started to sell. Her ambition wasn't for money; it was for her work to be acclaimed—for success! Not a lady painter's success, either, but real success, like Pollock's and De Kooning's—she wanted serious recognition by the serious world. The bitch-goddess Success. Who had called it that? She knew once. She'd heard it at a party long ago and laughed at the wit of the phrase.

Away from Jean's reassurances, she felt sick over her life. And where was Jean now? With which of his women? Up here in Vermont, alone (and I am alone, she thought), looking out at the mountains, breathing in the wet-leaf earth smell, she could finally, truly see it, as clearly as a memory: success as a painter was not coming for her.

The smell of smoke filtered through the air. She was cold, sitting on a rock near the pond, holding her empty cup. She had forgotten about Stephen, but now she saw him moving through the lit-up barn like a shadow puppet. He had put on Puccini (to please her? she wondered). The muffled music was grating in the wild mountain night.

Finally, Stephen opened the door and called to her. "Hey, Sheila, aren't you getting cold? Dinner's ready."

THEY ATE A LAMB STEW THAT STEPHEN HAD COOKED IN A SWEET, thick red-wine gravy full of onions and carrots, slices of turnip, a bay leaf. Every piece of meat was tender and rich-tasting in her mouth. It was very good, and she knew he had troubled over it for her. They were drinking a bottle of Uncle Toby's wine that was unlike any she had ever tasted. The wine was soft with a trace of clove, lovely, smooth in her mouth, slipping down her throat.

"Where's that from?" she asked, pointing her fork at the banner that loomed over the dinner table: ALL MEN ARE BROTH-ERS.

"I'm not sure. I think Toby got it at auction. I think—I be-lieve it's a flag Mother Jones marched with."

"I see," Sheila said, and smiled up at the banner, at its painted-on letters that were crackled from age, at the impossible, sweet hope they represented, encased on the wall like a dead wildflower pressed between wax-paper sheets. Had Stephen's cousin bought it for himself, as a reminder? Or was it only a cu-riosity, like the spinning wheel and the antique wool cards he had

displayed around the barn? Mother Jones's sign made Sheila sad.
She turned away from it.

Stephen was talking about anthropology, about the trip he was
going on in May. She'd love to go on a trip like that, she thought
idly, seeing Stephen so lit up. I shouldn't be here, she thought. I
am not the woman for him. How strange that he was so insanely
wealthy. She couldn't fathom it.

"Would you take some photos of the women in the tribe for
me?"

Stephen smiled. "Yes, absolutely. I'm planning on taking
loads of still pictures, black-and-white and color. In fact, I want
to put together a photo book when I get back."

"And a book book, too. You *are* going to write a book about
the whole thing? Your trip and experiences and the people? You
should take a portable typewriter."

Stephen looked at her. He was frowning, thinking; she could
see it. Didn't he realize he was a writer underneath it all? Not
just another art-collecting Hesse? Was he just discovering that
he was his own person? The letters he had sent her that fall were
perfectly crafted, beautiful things. Some of them were like
poems. What a curse his name was. How would anyone be able
to see his writing through the glare from a billion gold coins?
And isn't it funny, Sheila thought. He really is gifted. How much
better off would he be if he had been born poor? she wondered.

"Yes, write a book, Stephen. Take photos so you can remember everything when you get back."

If only she were a different person, or younger maybe. She
could see how easy it would be to fall madly in love with Stephen
Hesse.

He shook his head. "I don't want to write travel memoirs. I

want to study the people from an anthropological, a *scientific,* perspective. I want to help my professor record the war rituals. And I'm way too junior to write a paper about the fieldwork we're going to conduct. I won't even be a graduate student yet. Besides, I'm going to have my hands full collecting artifacts for the Hesse Museum and helping to build the photographic record for Professor Adams."

Sheila didn't say anything. But he would write his book—she knew it; she could smell his ambition to write like she could smell paint on a painter.

SHEILA AND STEPHEN WASHED THE DISHES AND DRANK THE REST of the delicious wine. He was adoring again, bounding on top of her with a boyish, puppyish physical affection laced with sexual aggressiveness that left her no room but to receive him, passive and brooding. She got out of bed after Stephen fell asleep, and smoked a cigarette. The telephone in the pantry beckoned her. She picked up the receiver and listened to the dial tone. But why call? He wasn't there.

She grabbed a mohair blanket off the couch and went outside into the cold night. A three-quarter moon glowed. She sat down on the flagstones and looked out at the world. A black cloud of bats, tiny, mouse-size bats, flew out from the nearby trees and crossed the pond. She was so blue. She hated the expensively renovated, gloomy barn. Even the bats flying past her silhouetted in the moonlit clouds made her sorry. She felt bad about Stephen. She shouldn't have taken up with him so lightly just because he intrigued her, just to distract herself from her constant upset over Jean's affairs.

Stephen was remarkable, she thought. He was emerging from the cocoon; the dust pattern on his wings was fragile. It was her mistake. She was so much older than him, so uninterested in taking him on. She knew that she was the first woman he'd ever slept with. But then she stopped thinking about Stephen. Her mind's eye wandered back to the mountains, to the sweet smell of the night air. She missed Jean. She always did.

Sheila was awake all night. At dawn, she made coffee and opened a can of condensed milk. It was a clear day. The wind that blew over the mountains was cold and pure. She went back out to her perch to watch the day emerge into the sky. She looked up and saw Stephen standing there, leaning in the doorway, haloed by the early morning sunlight.

"My God." He smiled at her. "You're as beautiful as a dream, Sheila."

      ✿     ✿     ✿

STEPHEN HAD WOKEN UP SLOWLY TO THE DAY POURING THROUGH the windows. The smell of brewing coffee entered him before consciousness took over. He lay in bed and felt sleep lingering in his neck, along his spine, in his eyelids. Finally, he got out of bed and wandered into the kitchen. Where was Sheila? he wondered, sleepy, happy. He found the sugar bag, coffee grains spilled in a trail across the counter, a spoon in the sink.

He walked to the door and stretched his arms wide, stood on his toes. The day was perfect New England autumn: cool and clear, white puffed-out clouds, blue sky over the mountains. There she was. Beautiful. Golden brown, her full breasts under her sweater, soft, smooth skin. But she was so far away from him.

He watched her all through breakfast and when she walked over to the pond while he packed up the house and his bags of books. She dipped her fingers in the water and stood up to look out. Stephen's whole body yearned for her. He wanted to run outside, spread her down on the ground and smell her, run his fingers along her body, up under her sweater, down into her pants, demand that she tell him she loved him.

He got his sketchbook and followed her. She was lying in the grass, looking up at the sky.

"Hmm, the clouds," she murmured. "They are incredible."

Stephen lined up his colored pencils in the tin. He sketched her profile; her lovely ears and then her hair, a dark blond cloud beneath her. He drew her gray sweater, her pink slacks stretched over strong legs, imagining her body, her breasts, under her clothes.

> I wandered lonely as a cloud
> That floats on high o'er vales and hills,
> When all at once I saw a crowd,
> A host, of golden daffodils

"That's so lovely," Sheila said. She closed her eyes and turned her face to the sun.

"My mother made me memorize that poem when I was young."

"Do you remember any more of it?"

"I don't know. Maybe. I'd like to draw you nude."

"Oh, would you?"

"No, really. I mean it."

"Mmm," Sheila said. "I see, a whole *Déjeuner sur l'herbe* thing, huh? Well, forget it. It's way too cold to *sur* in the herbs today."

Stephen laughed and kissed her and left her lying in the sun while he finished packing up the car.

HE DROVE QUICKLY ALL THE WAY DOWN FROM VERMONT, BUT EVEN so, they weren't in the city until the following afternoon. Stephen was full of foreboding about parting with Sheila. The fact that she was so close, sitting less than an arm's length from him, her smell and her face filling up the car, made him feel worse and worse. Every mile he drove seemed more difficult than the one before. He thought he'd never see her again; or at least that he'd never be alone with her again. He forced her—he felt he forced her—to agree to see him when he was down from school. But she wouldn't come up to Cambridge, or visit Haleyville; she didn't want go back up to Uncle Toby's barn. She told him again that she had only recently split up with Jean. She didn't want a new boyfriend; she wanted to paint.

It was raining in the city. Stephen drove down to her apartment on West Eleventh Street. He had assumed that he'd stay with her that night, that he'd leave in the morning to drive up to school from her place, but it was clear that she didn't want him to stay. It felt as though they'd never been away together. Vermont, their intimacy, was a dream. Cold, brown, raining New York was what was real. The city always woke him up and brought him back to his life. They sat in the car while the rain drummed away on the roof and slid down the windshield.

"What about Thanksgiving? I'll be down at Thanksgiving."

"Okay," she said, smiling at him, sanguine. "I'll look forward to it."

"Can I write to you from school?"

"Jesus, Stephen, you don't have to ask me. Just do it. You

know I love your letters. Write, don't write—do whatever you want."

She stroked his cheek with the back of her hand. He fought the urge to push her away. You don't love me, he thought. He could hit her; right then he wanted to smack her. The rain was pouring hard; the car windows were fogging up. Stephen looked at the hood of the car, expecting to see sleet bouncing off it. Sheila kissed him and ran from the car, through the rain, to the door of her apartment building. He watched her fish her keys out of her purse and open the front door. And then she was gone.

# 7

# IN THE HIGHLANDS

I T WAS LATE MAY. SUMMER WAS ALREADY BREATHING WARM, humid air into Cambridge, Massachusetts, as Harvard's groundskeepers swept up after the university's graduation festivities. But on the other side of the world, in the Southern Hemisphere, the Western New Guinea Highlands were in the midst of a rainy season, which reminded the newly arrived Harvard University anthropological team of early spring back home: spring, but more so. Twice daily, raging downpours soaked the mountains, and at night it was so cold they could see their breath.

The two youngest members of the team, Stephen Hesse and John Nightingale, started for home one evening, trekking up into the foothills of Mount Karamui. They'd been working all day in Koa village, and they were hungry and tired but still fired up. They walked up a steep, narrow path that was cut through thickets of sharp-leaved wild sugarcane surrounded by the dying day—wet, cold Highlands air, the smell of woodsmoke and mud and pig shit, the cicadas screaming. Shivering clouds of black fruit bats hovered over the trees. Stephen stopped and looked out at the expanse of rainforest-covered mountains that were blue in the fading light.

"Isn't it awful to think of all this paved over and destroyed? Full of electric lights and cement-block houses? All Westernized and poor?" Stephen asked.

"Why think of it the way it isn't? This is what it is now," Nightingale answered.

"Because it's what's coming. The West will suck this place in and spew it out ugly and poor instead of beautiful and primeval."

"No one knows what's to be, Stephen, and who can tell what'll be after him? The future is just a fairy tale made up by people in the present. The only real thing is now. This moment."

"Just wait, John," Stephen said, frowning. "Just wait and see what happens here if nothing is done to protect the land."

"And what're you going to do? Put up a gate to keep out the Wicked Witch of the West? Don't be so gloomy, young man. I'd wager that this"—Nightingale gestured out at the mountains—"will be here long after both of us've been returned into dust."

Nightingale was English; stocky, with light brown hair and wire-rimmed glasses over pure blue eyes. He was a graduate student in the anthropology department at Harvard. He and Stephen had been assigned the grunt work for the team. They spent most of their days mapping out the Koa River valley, with its villages and tall, spindly watchtowers, the deserted ghost houses, the tiny hamlets along the ridges of Mount Karamui. They cataloged the trees, bushes, plants and flowers that grew around the human settlements, the small marsupials that crawled through the forest, the pythons and orchids, the bower birds and insects; the Ulysses butterflies, as big as small birds, that hovered in clearings, their enormous wings shimmering blue as they settled on a leaf.

In the four weeks since they had arrived in the field, Hesse and Nightingale had mapped the faraway kitchen gardens that spread sweet-potato ivy and banana trees over the slope of the mountain wall. They had walked deep into the rainforest to the groundwater pools where the village women soaked up brine in strips of banana trunk and then lay them in the sun to dry and become salt. Stephen wanted to publish a book of photographs when he got back to New York, and Nightingale helped him, holding the flashes, the light meter and the gray card, labeling rolls of Kodak film as fast as Stephen shot them.

He took the photographs that Sheila had asked him for: women working in their gardens, nursing their babies, laughing together. But he took these pictures when he was by himself, as though just photographing the images she wanted evoked her presence.

HESSE AND NIGHTINGALE HAD BEGUN TO KNOW THE KOA VIL-lagers. At first, only the boy children befriended them: skinny, naked little things, with protruding bellies and scrawny legs covered in pus-filled tropical ulcers, their deep brown eyes full of curiosity and humor as they ran beside Hesse and Nightingale, touching them, chattering away. But soon older men, men their own age, were acknowledging them, nodding their heads as the two researchers made their way among them, tromping through hamlets, loaded down with cameras and recording equipment.

By the end of the second week in the Highlands, Hesse and Nightingale had a pocketful of names that went with faces: Biri, Jao, Malau, Tindano. The men their age were warriors—muscular, short, brown-skinned men, their bodies gleaming black from the pig fat mixed with ashes that they rubbed all over their skin and into their hair. They were naked except for their penis gourds and the delicately woven shell chest-pieces and the reed bracelets that encircled their wrists and upper arms.

STEPHEN ADMIRED HOW JOHN NIGHTINGALE WAS SO COMFORTABLE with the New Guineans. Sometimes he even sank into fits of dark envy over it. John was so smart. His mind was clear. Everything—ideas, understanding, an ease of manner—seemed a part of him. He didn't have to work at it. When they left Koa village at the end of the day (loaded down like infantrymen, with rucksacks full of cameras and film, tape recorders, books, notebooks, first-aid kits, canteens of purified water), they half ran up the steep mountain path, gulping in the thin air and talking.

They talked about ideas and books: Malinowski, Lévi-Strauss, Marx. They talked and talked, arguing, insistent, until Stephen couldn't keep up with Nightingale and he became tortured by their conversation. He felt as if there was something missing in himself, something that was very much there in Nightingale. He thought of the difference between their minds in physical terms, as if John could leap higher or run farther and faster than him. He was just smarter. Stephen envied John, but he admired him more. Stephen looked up to the Englishman; and they had fun. Before they went to sleep, they read out loud chapters of *Under the Volcano* to each other. They even made plans to travel in Mexico. During the day they'd quote lines from Lowry's book to make each other smile.

" 'Brutal-looking candelabra cactus swung past, a ruined church, full of pumpkins, windows bearded with grass'!" Stephen growled.

"Full of pumpkins, yourself, Yankee."

THAT NIGHT HESSE AND NIGHTINGALE SLOWED AS THEY AP-proached the top of Mount Karamui. A tiny hamlet of three huts sat a few hundred feet down the path from the research house. Stephen had taken almost a hundred photographs of the place. Scraggy banana trees, smoke-blackened thatch roofs covered in flowering weeds, sleeping pigs on flat red sun-warmed earth, the endless cloud forest that spread out on the horizon. Only a few old men and women and quiet children lived in the isolated lit-tle hamlet. The fathers, husbands and sons were either living in the men's house down in the village or had been killed in battle. There was something in this corner of the Koa Valley that was impossibly beautiful to Stephen. It was so full of feeling, as lonely as the end of the world.

Hesse and Nightingale leaned on the pig fence, looking in through one of the huts' open doors. They watched the hearth fire burning red, yellow-orange flames against the darkness; blue smoke seeping up from the thatch. Soft night was slowly pouring in around them, filling up the mountains. They could see a woman in the glow of the flames. She pulled a sweet-potato tuber out of the ashes, banged it on the mud floor to loosen the skin from its steaming white meat. Nightingale looked over at Stephen.

"Isn't the firelight amazing?" he said.

"It's unbelievable," Stephen breathed, gazing at the scene unfolding in front of him: the woman peeling her sweet potato, the smell of the smoke in the mountain air. "It's so *so* unbelievable."

They walked away from the little hamlet, and the night, the mountains, the vision of the small flames, beset Stephen. He listened to the sound of their hiking boots on the mud path and the cicadas screaming in the bush around them. He was excited almost every moment in New Guinea; right then he was so full of nervous tingling that he worried he'd burst out laughing. He blocked everything from his mind and searched the dark for the lights of the research house.

※      ※      ※

THE RESEARCH HOUSE SAT NEXT TO AN AIRFIELD ON THE UPPER reaches of Mount Karamui, in the central highlands of Netherlands New Guinea, at about latitude 4° south and longitude 138°50′ east. The crudely cut airfield looked down at the Koa Valley and the mountain wall that formed its barrier to the west. The house was two stories high, constructed six months before the Harvard team arrived. It was built from woven bamboo, split eucalyptus and a corrugated aluminum roof that had been helicoptered up from Washkul station.

Inside, on the first floor, smooth river rocks paved the damp earth, and in the kitchen a two-burner stove sat on a table, hooked up to a propane drum. Rough-hewn shelves were stacked with tins of jack mackerel, tuna, stewed goose, curried duck, condensed milk, powdered eggs, canvas bags of rice and sugar, tins of tea and glass jars of Nescafé and Tiptree jam. A wide window looked out onto the quiet airfield. During the day, the team kept it open and watched the araucaria and pandanus trees quiver in the mountaintop winds.

Stephen and John shared the upstairs—Professor Adams and his friend James Gwathmey, along with Erich Van Gropius, an anthropologist the Dutch colonial government had sent to join them, lived on the first floor, in small private rooms off the kitchen. The upstairs was open space, full of the smell of smoke-dried thatch and bamboo, camera gear and books scattered across the floor and the two young men's cots, covered in rumpled sleeping bags and army blankets, at either end of the room.

Stephen wanted to collect artifacts for the Hesse Museum. Nicholas had refused to give him guidelines. "Buy what you like," his father had said. "It's the only way to get anything good." So Stephen bought objects from the Koa villagers for the museum—net bags, bird-hunting arrows, two decorated shields, some cowrie-shell bands, feathered and furred headbands, a stone adze—and these were all stacked in a corner, tagged in neatly handwritten labels.

From his cot, Stephen could push open a window and watch the sun rise. Sometimes the equatorial sun arrived behind a wall of rain-filled clouds, sometimes slow and pinkish-red, turning the gray sky a ruddy orange color. He saw the rain-fat clouds on the trees beyond the muddy, grassy plain of the airfield, turning to light mist as the sun came full in the sky and burned them away.

And the rain. He had never known anything like the rain in the Highlands—violent, insistent, beating the roof like a drum all night, beating down on Stephen and John Nightingale, catching them while they were out photographing, roaming from hamlet to hamlet, exploring the brine pools and the mile-wide kitchen gardens. Hard, fat raindrops, one after another, melting the sweet-smelling black earth into pools of muddy clay, swelling to bursting the rivers that crashed down the mountainside, ripping apart the rope bridges that spanned their banks.

The sun set so slowly on some days it was as if it didn't want to leave the mountains at all, and the twilight lasted even after John and Stephen were back from the village and had eaten a dinner of curried duck and rice and drunk endless cups of tea.

Lying in his cot, Stephen wrote long letters to his father. So far from home, Stephen felt closer to his father than he ever had. He carried Nicholas with him everywhere. He told his father that the Highlands reminded him of Mount Desert Island, with a climate of eternal springtime, only landlocked. It was funny how much New Guinea reminded him of Maine. Marguerite floated through him as he wrote to his father. But he didn't write to her. He didn't know what to say.

He wrote to Sheila and sent her ink drawings of the village, of women walking home from the gardens, loaded down with net bags of sweet-potato tubers and sugarcane. He had pasted a photograph of Sheila into his notebook and surrounded it with pencil drawings of plants and orchids that grew in the rainforest. He dreamed about her; she filled his nights with her warm, soft body, her wet mouth; he awoke in the cold, quiet Highlands night without her, and masturbated. Even in the middle of the day, if he closed his eyes, he could smell the linseed oil on her hands, see the sun-shadow patterns on the floor of her house on Fire Island.

✿          ✿          ✿

THERE WAS, OF COURSE, A STRAINED, CAREFUL MANNER AMONG the four of them from Harvard. Every one of them except for Hesse had experience, training, so much knowledge. Stephen was a child to them. He had only just graduated from the college. He was there because of who he was. Because quietly, almost secretly, Nicholas Hesse had funded the Harvard anthropological expedition when his son asked him to; he had even made a series of telephone calls to Amsterdam to ensure Dutch cooperation. Governor Hesse had made Professor Adams's dream of studying and filming ritual warfare in the remote, almost unknown Highlands of Netherlands New Guinea—a task that could easily have taken the professor himself five years (if ever) to accomplish—happen with a wave of his wand. And so Professor Laird Adams, only thirty-five but already famous in his field, gave a coveted spot on his advance team to the governor's son. A place on this tiny, historic team of white men who had traveled sideways through time to an untouched Neolithic culture nestled in an exquisite rainforest valley. A culture full of magic, ritual cannibalism and warfare; of rival tribesmen, who had been killing one another through the millennia. Men who chopped down trees with stone adzes and hunted marsupial opossum and birds of paradise with bow and arrow, women who nursed piglets at their breasts alongside their babies and sang lullabies and fertility spells to the sweet-potato tubers that grew in the rich black Highlands soil. The Koa Valley was untouched in 1961, rarer than anything any white man would ever encounter again.

Professor Adams and his friend James Gwathmey, a Boston Brahmin, a thin, watery man, a naturalist and Harvard alumnus, a novelist who would become famous as a writer of books about exotic animals and faraway places, felt awkward around the governor's son. They couldn't really look at him, or at the rat's nest of feelings—protectiveness, envy, resentment, indebtedness, embarrassment—he provoked in them. And in the intimacy of the research house Stephen couldn't hide the arrogance of wealth that rested on his skin. He was the eldest son of one of the richest, most powerful men in the United States, in the world, and it was no use pretending otherwise, although he tried. But at the same time, Stephen intuited, with a kind of savant accuracy, just how much conflict his presence generated in his professor and James Gwathmey; in these two men he wanted to be like, in these two men he wanted so much to be accepted by.

Stephen was deposited with John Nightingale, upstairs, to dwell on the perimeter of the team, kept farther away than even the foreign, unknown Van Gropius. But he was lucky in his roommate, Nightingale, the brilliant British graduate student, who would in the not too distant future also become famous, albeit to a much lesser degree than Gwathmey.

Nightingale had grown up in a genteel but relentlessly shabby poverty until he was sent to a posh boys' public school, Christ's Hospital, on a scholarship. He was the poor boy at Christ's Hospital; the poor, handsome, talented boy sprouted from an undistinguished family of shopkeepers and schoolteachers. Nightingale spent his boyhood, his adolescence, sleeping and eating, learning and playing sports, fighting, bleeding, pissing and shitting, side by side with boys who could find their surnames in William's Domesday Book, boys who would inherit titles and castles and unfathomable wealth.

But poor John Nightingale's mind outpaced theirs; he felt things in the poetry they were made to memorize, in the history, philosophy, chemistry, in the Latin and mathematics, that they couldn't. Eventually, his supple mind arrived at a vantage point that offered him a startlingly clear view—everything, *everything* they were taught, even Christ on Calvary and the things that went unspoken, like position and class, was part of a pattern, part of an endless system created by men to make sense of the world.

But the world itself didn't care what they thought up—it was forever remote, unknowable, chaotic, arbitrary. It was the thrill of that understanding, as well as the knowledge of his own talent, that protected him from the horrors of being a charity case, that allowed his psyche to develop and his soul to unfurl as he became a young man.

So John Nightingale was unthreatened by the young multimillionaire in a way that the two older men, the Americans, couldn't be. It wasn't that Nightingale was blind to the power of the Hesse money, or that he wasn't enraged by the unfairness; the immutability of caste, money, power and title were engraved on his heart from before he could speak. But, still, he was unafraid. He was even seduced by Stephen's openness, by the feeling in his brown eyes.

Even years later the English anthropologist's heart would break as he thought about those early weeks in the field that were full of Hesse's exuberance. In a way, the young American was so alive to the unexpected, overwhelming beauty of the Highlands that he had revealed it to all of them.

THE NEXT DAY, STEPHEN WOKE TO SOFT RAIN DRUMMING ON THE roof. Jao and Tindano showed up at the research house at dawn, emerging from the mist and clouds outside, wet and somber.

They were on their way to the "true bush," they said, squatting by the stove, smoking tobacco in bamboo pipes, while Stephen boiled water for tea. They were going high, they told him, into the forest above Mount Karamui, to gather special flowers for a magic rite to heal their friend, a young warrior named Ebabome, who was very sick. Professor Adams had declared that Ebabome was dying from tetanus, but everyone in Koa thought he'd been shot with a poisoned arrow by an enemy tribe across the valley.

Professor Adams, Gwathmey, Nightingale and even Van Gropius had been to Ebabome's mother's hut, where the dying teenager lay in smoky darkness, curled on his side. The rictus made his face into a pitiful, emaciated grimace looming in the daylight that streamed in from the doorway. However, unlike the rest of the team, Stephen had visited him again and again, almost every time he was down in the village, as though there were something in Ebabome's hut for him.

He was revolted by the stink of human sickness, but he was fascinated, too. He would come in, ducking under the hut's short doorway, and sit against the woven-bamboo wall, hugging his legs to his chest, silent, embarrassed at his own ghoulishness. The hearth fire smoldered, filling the air with its smoky, sooty taste. Soon his eyes adjusted to the dark and he felt Ebabome staring at him. Sometimes Stephen saw curiosity burning in his eyes. But then the young warrior's sickness, his awful pain, reclaimed him and his gaze returned to emptiness and drifted toward the light outside the door.

Stephen watched Ebabome's mother rocking back and forth in the smoky shadows, moaning, while furry brown rats crawled lazily through the thatch roof, down along the walls into the shadows under the sleeping platforms. A sow slept by the doorway, snorting and gruffling. Ebabome's younger sister chewed sugarcane bark and spit the juice into an old tin for her brother. Ebabome's mother and sister rarely looked at Stephen. His presence seemed unremarkable to them, as if he were a stray dog that had wandered in, looking for shade from the noonday sun.

Eventually, Stephen didn't mind the smell of the musky, smoky sweat and urine, the yellow diarrhea that Ebabome's mother wiped from him with banana leaves. He didn't understand his own fascination with the place, with Ebabome, but then he didn't try to. He wrote every detail of his visits in his notebook and drew the sad little fatherless family waiting in their dark hut for the man-child to die.

So that morning when Ebabome's friends showed up on their way to the summit of Mount Karamui, Stephen wanted to go with them. He wanted to go alone, too—he didn't wake up Nightingale or tell Adams. He packed his camera bag with the Leica and extra film, a rain poncho, chocolate bars, matches and his canteen.

The three of them drank down their sweet, steaming-hot tea and walked away from the research house in silence, in the drizzle, across the airfield, up onto a path that led into a grove of tall eucalypts. Soon they were walking through light secondary-growth forest, surrounded by the rain dripping on the leaves, the shrill cries of birds of paradise, of insects buzzing, the smell of water-drenched earth and moss and bark.

They were hiking, trekking higher and higher, and the air became very thin. The two men slowed down for Stephen, who was out of breath and stunned by the high forest. Up only a few hundred feet from the research house the rainforest was full of a diffuse, wet greenish-yellow light that he had never seen before. Vines drooped to the moss-carpeted floor; brilliant orange-and-purple orchids grew next to thin saplings, incandescent splashes in the blur of green. And the sound of life! Everything was so alive: the hum of thousands of birds, the hypnotic sound of rain dripping through the tree canopy.

Stephen realized that Nightingale was right. The present was all that was true, this moment that was breathing in the future and exhaling the past. Everything else besides it was a dream, a ghost, nonexistent. He was standing in the midst of all that was real.

Stephen felt alive in Koa in a way that he never had before—sensually alive, with his thoughts trailing after his feelings. The sun, the afternoon rains, the moon, had seeped inside him, into his blood. His thoughts were like clouds drifting across the sky, there if he wanted to look but soft, undemanding. What mattered was the heat of the sun on his skin, the taste of wild mushrooms roasted in bamboo tubes, tinned mackerel mixed into sticky, glutinous rice balls, salty and delicious.

But that morning in the high rainforest with Jao and Tindano, Stephen discovered that his mind was sharper than it had been since he left the States. He saw himself: he saw that his soul was quivering in response to New Guinea. But he also saw that deep at the bottom of himself a lonely, sorry feeling was knocking around like a moth flying up against a lit-up window at night. What is wrong with me? he thought, and an ache spread through his chest and tightened around his heart. He saw the frantic missing and wanting of Sheila that he kept bandaged so tightly in his body. He hadn't expected this sudden clarity high up in the mountains, and he didn't want it. He willed it away, letting the soft, narcotic beauty of the rainforest, its heady smell, enter his lungs and seep into his blood, his mind, until his senses reasserted themselves over his being.

Soon they were walking in real cloud forest. It was quieter, with only the rustle of slow-moving possums and tree kangaroos, a bird of paradise calling in the distance. Stephen couldn't have a true conversation with Jao and Tindano; he understood so little of the Koa language. He wondered what they thought of him. Did he seem ugly to them? Was he unreal? These men were nicer to him than anyone on the trip except Nightingale. And they were the only ones who treated him as an equal. Wasn't it something that he had to travel the farthest corners of the earth to find men who could see him? Stephen allowed himself a moment of self-pity. He hated the awkwardness at the research house with Adams and Gwathmey; even Van Gropius always seemed to be laughing behind his hand. He wouldn't be sorry to say good-bye to them.

Stephen looked up ahead at Jao and Tindano. He watched their strong legs, saw their wide, muscular bare feet slap on the moss, over slick logs. They were, all three of them, he thought, at that moment the same. Three men, three animals, climbing ever farther into the cloud forest, heading up and up even as the air thinned out, determined, as though they were going to march right up into the sky itself.

As they stood at an elevation of twelve thousand feet and looked down at the green girdling the great valley that spread below, an old poem, a poem that he had loved through a summer up in Mount Desert Island, floated through his mind.

> *Oh, lift me as a wave, a leaf, a cloud!*
> *I fall upon the thorns of life! I bleed*

Jao stopped. He had found the precious flowers for Ebabome growing from a vine. They were pinkish-red urn-shaped flowers, waxy, and the forest floor was covered with them. They smelled sweet to Stephen, like a ripe pear. He photographed the men as they gathered the flowers, filling two net bags to bursting with the blossoms. He photographed the mountain wall through the trees and drank a sip of tinny-tasting water from his canteen. As they walked back, the morning mist turned into heavy rain.

When Stephen got back, he burst into the research house soaking wet and covered in mud, with twigs sticking out of his hair, blood-fat leeches lolling in his socks, and his jacket pockets overflowing with the magic red flowers. Nightingale came downstairs, smiling, to see Stephen looking like a creature swallowed and spit up by the rainforest. It was an image he would always remember of the heir to the Hesse fortune.

# 8

## THE PYRE

A LITTLE AFTER ONE THE NEXT MORNING A WEIRD, HIGH-pitched wailing, as disturbing and unexpected as an ambulance siren, rang through the Koa Valley, up into its forests, echoed off the mountain wall and flew up the steep, muddy path to the top of Mount Karamui. Stephen woke up afraid. The smell of coffee filled the upstairs. Nightingale was still asleep. Stephen saw light through the cracks in the woven-bamboo floor and went down to the kitchen. Professor Adams was pouring Nescafé and condensed milk into their five thermoses. Gwathmey sat illuminated by a kerosene lantern hanging from the ceiling, his long legs crossed, smoking a cigarette.

Adams handed Stephen a cup of coffee. It was delicious: sweet and hot and strong.

"He'll be famous in death, our young Ebabome," Gwathmey

said. "Studied by the generations of undergraduates in Anthro
101."

"Did he die?" Stephen asked, feeling foolish.

"Can't you hear it?" Gwathmey asked, and waved his cigarette toward the window, toward the distant sound of the high-
pitched cries.

"You'd better wake up Nightingale," Professor Adams said.
"We're going to leave for the village."

Of course Ebabome had died; he was so sick. Wasn't that
why they were interested in him? Wasn't it why *he* was interested in Ebabome? *Because* he was going to die? Why should
Stephen feel frightened and sorry right then as he walked back
upstairs to wake Nightingale? But he did.

The five of them walked through the lonely blue night
toward the dirge. They were carrying cameras and flashes, sound
equipment, the tripods and Adams's eight-millimeter movie
camera. Gwathmey had his canvas first-aid bag strapped across
his chest, its red-painted cross facing out. What danger was he
preparing for? Stephen wondered. What would that little bag
full of rolled gauze bandages, iodine and a packet of cigarettes
protect him from, exactly?

Torches and small fires burned in the courtyard of Koa's
main hamlet. In the half-lit dark it looked as though there were
hundreds of people. Stephen couldn't recognize anyone at first,
and then gradually, like in a dream, familiar faces floated past
him, lit up for a moment and then faded back into the darkness.
None of the Koa seemed to notice the team, not even when
Adams set up the bright lamps for filming and Stephen's camera
hissed flashes of white light.

Night bled into a murky, clouded-over dawn. Gwathmey and

Adams weaved in and out of the crowd of mourners, taking notes, holding the microphone up to catch their sounds. Still no one noticed the white men, or if they did, they didn't care enough to look at them. It occurred to Stephen that they were like ghosts, like shades floating among the Koa, hovering, hungry for them, trying to capture the life, the blood warmth, of recent death that was unfolding in front of them.

Nightingale handed him a cup of coffee and a wheat biscuit. Stephen ate, but he wasn't hungry. He kept photographing, occasionally stopping to jot a note to himself in his journal. While he was helping Nightingale set up tape recorders and microphones, he saw that hidden behind the long, rectangular men's house four men were building a chair out of wood planks. When he began taking pictures, they glanced up for a moment and then went back to ignoring him. The chairmakers argued with one another and smoked for an hour before they finally lashed the seat together. When they were done, a rough-hewn throne with a high back and stilt legs stood under a banana tree behind the men's house.

Finally, Ebabome was carried into the early morning. The women sitting in the courtyard became frenzied; their chanting dirge turned back into the uncanny wailing that had woken Stephen up. The dead boy had been prepared carefully for his funeral: his emaciated body and hair were coated in dyed pig fat so that even in the dull light he gleamed a deep, wet red.

The throne had been moved into the center of the courtyard, and the chairmakers sat Ebabome in it, lashing a string around his chest and placing a wood plank under his knees so that his head and shoulders drooped over into a fetal position. The sun burned through the early morning mist. People from faraway hamlets across the valley, from Ebabome's mother's village, began to arrive, swelling Koa into a sea of milling people.

Ebabome's uncles and the chairmakers adorned him with finery: long, knitted cowrie-shell bands, feathered and furred headbands, newly woven net bags. With each new treasure placed on Ebabome the women wailed, and a different man stood up and gave a speech. The women, covered in ashes, their hair shorn, wearing necklaces of Job's tears, all sitting, grouped to the throne's left, were like a chorus in an ancient Greek tragedy, moaning strophe and antistrophe, punctuating the men's speeches, the activity, the still morning air, with the relentless fact of death in front of them.

There was Ebabome, arrayed in his family's riches, his head nodded over his chest as though he were asleep. He was there, just the same as he had been in his hut the day before. Stephen could see the cracked skin on the soles of his feet, dried mud on his ankles. How queer it was to have physical death so close. Were these the gates of death revealed? Were the gates of deep darkness nothing, after all?

"They're driving away his ghost, you see," Professor Adams whispered to Stephen, pointing at two men shooting arrows into a bundle of grass. "Be sure you get photographs of all of that."

Stephen felt his professor's excitement: Adams was finding gold in a riverbed, catching the rarest of butterflies in his net.

"Definitely," he said, and picked up his Leica.

"You see, everything right now is being done to appease the ancestor-ghosts, and especially Ebabome's ghost, which is *fresh*, so it's in its most powerful, malevolent state. So everything"—Adams pointed to several pigs that were tied to the fence, waiting for slaughter—"you see, *everything* they are doing right now is to appease his ghost."

Two of the chairmakers had begun a pyre, a roaring fire blazing in the now-full sun of a pure blue sky morning. The women's wailing became howls of *aiyee aiyeee aiyee* as the treasures were slowly removed from Ebabome and punctiliously rolled up and put away. After all his clan's wealth had been removed, Ebabome was carried in his throne by the chairmakers and hoisted onto the fire. Again the women wailed as the flames ate the chair, and soon a burned-skin-and-hair smell flooded the compound. But Ebabome sat still as his pyre burned.

Stephen's mind jumped around as he watched the flames. Unbidden, random thoughts of his great-grandfather, of Sheila, of his mother, swirled through his mind. He was nailed to the spot by the sight of the flames burning Ebabome's body. How horrible that it all ended with dust and ashes. If a man dies, will he live again? It seemed like such a silly question all of a sudden. At that moment, the young warrior's ghost was realer to Stephen than any thought of Christ. The column of smoke from Ebabome's pyre reached up to the beautiful Highlands sky. Remember that my life is a breath.

Stephen's reverie was broken by pigs squealing. The chairmakers were killing the tied-up pigs for the feast, shooting them in the neck with a bow and arrow and then slicing through pale pink fat to their jugular arteries with bamboo knives. Finally the too-close morning sun, the blue-red pig's blood flowing onto the ground, the chorus of women moaning, the smell of Ebabome burning on his pyre, was too much. Stephen felt horrible. He began hallucinating that he was drifting up out of his body. He fainted.

When he woke up, he was cradled in Nightingale's arms.

"You all right?"

"I'm fine, I'm fine."

"It's a lot, all of this. It's tough stuff, isn't it?" Nightingale shook his head. Stephen felt the man's warmth and kindness. There was a richness to John Nightingale's soul. "It's certainly more real, more human than anything I've ever seen."

"I'm okay, John." Stephen sat up and pushed Nightingale's arms away, an adolescent struggling out of his mother's embrace. "I just had a moment."

A flush of red shame filled him. Had everyone seen him?

"It's like there's no filter here, no barriers to unadulterated humanity in all its grotesque and divine incarnations," Nightingale continued. "You and I are from a culture that's spent thousands of years devising ways to protect itself from the un-bearable animal fact of death. And then, all of a sudden, here it is. Here it is."

Stephen couldn't understand John. He was too upset and embarrassed. The pounding in his ears was loud. He was afraid he would pass out again.

They stayed sitting, the two of them, while the pyre burned down to smoldering ashes and smoke-blackened wood. Soon Ebabome's sister emerged from the group of mourning women and began sifting through the ashes with a pair of bamboo tongs.

"She's looking for his bones," John said.

"Ah, the Magdalene," Stephen murmured, unable to take his eyes off the girl, her face and body covered in white ashes, her head shaved and caked with black mud; she was beautiful to him.

"Come again?" John asked.

"Nothing," Stephen said, and smiled at him.

Stephen took photographs of the girl as she plucked her brother's bones from the ashes and placed them gingerly on a wide banana leaf. They stayed in the village until the sun set, and then, exhausted, Hesse and Nightingale followed the rest of the team as they walked in silence back up to the research house.

BY THE BEGINNING OF SEPTEMBER THE HARVARD ADVANCE TEAM had been working in the Koa Valley for five months. Professor Adams decided that they needed a short break to return to the United States. He wanted to resupply their stores, develop film and sort out their accumulated mass of field notes, photographs, audiotapes and maps. Two medical anthropologists from Johns Hopkins were coming out to the field in January and Adams wanted to brief them.

But also, the professor wanted to get out of Koa himself. The team needed a rest, a few weeks back in the States. Not an overly long time, he thought, but enough for his crew to prepare for the next six months.

None of them expected young Hesse to come back. The fieldwork had gone from being a series of thrilling discoveries to the grind of routine. He seemed disappointed, too, in the lack of Koa art. Highlanders, the team had learned, expressed their creativity almost exclusively through body art—tattoos, makeup, costume and masks. Although parts of New Guinea were famous for their sculpture, the art in the Highlands was intangible, uncollectable. The only things for Stephen to buy, really, were trinkets, woven net bags and old weapons.

TWO DAYS BEFORE THE TEAM WAS SET TO FLY OUT OF THE FIELD, Nightingale and Van Gropius walked into the research house and found Stephen, alone, at the kitchen table with a human skull in front of him. The skull was colored bright red, its eye sockets black with coal, giving it an unreal, almost comical look. Nightingale understood at once: Hesse had bought Ebabome's skull.

" 'Alas, poor Yorick! I knew him, Horatio. A fellow of infinite jest, of most excellent fancy,' " Nightingale said in a low, mocking voice.

Stephen turned unseeing eyes on Nightingale and Van Gropius. He was lost; Nightingale knew this expression of his, sunk deep in the corners of thought. They had, all of them, been packing for three weeks, getting ready to leave. And in those past three weeks Stephen had begun buying whatever the villagers brought to him.

Koa men showed up before dawn and sat patiently outside the research house waiting to sell their net bags and shields, necklaces of dogs' teeth, bow and arrows, shell breast-pieces and feather headdresses: Stephen's pile of artifacts grew until it spilled out into the middle of the floor. Yet no matter how much he bought, he couldn't alleviate his agitation. Nightingale saw that Hesse wanted to go already, that he was chafing under Gwathmey and Adams like a pupil at the end of a long, boring class.

Just in the past few days Stephen had stopped hiding his antipathy to the two older men. He was always polite, always correct, ever the well-bred scion. But he had unstoppered his resentment of Gwathmey and Adams's genteel condescension and neglect. Hesse's dissatisfaction filtered through the woven-bamboo walls of the research house as distinctly as the musky, smoky smell of the artifacts he had bought.

Yet what did it matter how he behaved? His money freed him. How Nightingale envied it, that freedom. He didn't envy the money itself, what filthy lucre can buy: fine, beautiful objects, houses, cars, women. But to be outside the caste system that ruled life. Hesse needn't always be stuffing his true self back down his own throat as Nightingale did. Nightingale knew he would never escape the grip and slog of everyday life; he would never experience existence without the worry of money squirreled away in his mind. He could imagine what it was to be a Koa man more easily than he could fathom being born to Hesse's wealth. To be free. Nightingale envied Hesse that and admired it on him the way he admired the iridescent plumage on the birds of paradise that fluttered through the uppermost reaches of the rainforest canopy.

But right then, Nightingale and Van Gropius had just walked up from the village, and they were hot and thirsty and hungry for lunch. There was Stephen in front of them, sitting with his fingers around the skull, absorbed in it. Nightingale saw everything as clearly as if he were looking at a photograph.

The two men watched Hesse finger the skull delicately, almost fondling it. Stephen's hair had grown out since they had been in the field and hung in loose black curls down his neck. He was sunburned and freckled and, alone of the team, had grown an untrimmed beard. At that moment Hesse's unkemptness irritated Nightingale. It seemed so studied, like a woman returning from a holiday in Cap d'Antibes with a dark tan, a blue-striped jersey and a fisherman's cap.

"Perhaps," Nightingale said gently, masking his bristling anger, "it—rather, Ebabome's head—should stay here, with his family, in Koa. What do you think?"

"They sold it to me. His uncle brought it up here this morning and *asked* me to buy it."

"But of course it's not for sale, Stephen, don't you see that?"

"I don't agree. I'm taking it back to New York for the museum."

"Don't you understand where you are, man?"

Hesse didn't answer. Instead, in that moment, he shed the skin of Adams's acolyte, of Nightingale's equal, that he'd worn for the past five months and emerged as who he really was. He pulled the impermeable membrane of his wealth, his social class, down between them. He would not be told what to do. Unconsciously, Nightingale shook his head. He knew that for someone like him to be angry at someone like Stephen Hesse was tantamount to being angry at an actor in a film flickering on the screen in front of you. In the end, you were alone in the dark, your feelings churning, yearning for a connection with someone who wasn't real.

And hadn't he played along with Hesse, enjoying the American's youth and humor and enthusiasm, flattered, too, that someone as illustrious as Hesse wanted to be his friend? *The Prince and the Pauper* answered a powerful wish in the psyche, John Nightingale thought. But after all, it was a fairy tale.

Van Gropius had watched the exchange between Nightingale and Hesse quietly.

"You know," the Dutchman said, "if you really want good stuff, yes, art and such, you're in the wrong place, no? The Asmat is where it all is. In these mountains there's nothing too good. Your skull"—he shrugged his shoulders—"okay. But the Asmat, my God. They make such sculpture, huge ancestor poles—the *bisj,* they're called, canoes. The carving is the most beautiful primitive art in the world. Oh my God, you can't believe it. All the Dutch museums send people to collect Asmat carving. So incredible."

"I want to go," Stephen said.

"Oh sure, sure. You got to fly to Biak and charter a plane to the coast. Then you take a ferry up to the Asmat."

"Would you come, John?" Stephen asked, his wide brown eyes lit up with the thought of it.

Once bitten, twice shy. No, Nightingale wouldn't go with Stephen. Not now, when he couldn't pretend away what he'd be: a paid companion on a shopping trip. He was too proud. Anyway, a hot contempt for Hesse was rushing through him. But on the surface Nightingale was temperate as an English summer's day.

"No," he said, lying. "I have no interest in the Asmat. They're all headhunters anyway. It's a bit dicey down there."

"Oh yah. You want skulls? They got so many skulls down there for sale!" Van Gropius laughed.

"So, will you take me, Erich?" Stephen asked, without skipping a beat.

"Oh yah. Of course, of course, any time we'll go. I think before the monsoon, okay?"

"I can be back very soon. When does the monsoon start? When should I come back?"

Van Gropius shrugged his shoulders. "I think if you are here, you know, in a month or so, by October fifteenth maybe. We will be okay then."

Stephen nodded. "October is not a problem."

"I should think you two would want to wait until after the monsoon," Nightingale said quietly. "Is there such a rush, Stephen?"

"Well, I don't want to wait," Stephen said. "Unless you'd come with us then, John."

Nightingale laughed. "Me? I'm coming right back here, to Koa."

"Then we're off to the Asmat in October, right, Erich?"

"Oh yah, yah. October is not too late."

"Well, *vaya con Dios*," Nightingale said, unable to keep the spite out of his voice.

He walked away as Hesse began to quiz Van Gropius about the settlements along the Asmat River. The image of Hesse and Van Gropius alone, prowling the interior, searching for carvings, right as the monsoon was about to hit, didn't sit well. Van Gropius seemed like a bit of a twit to him. Nightingale had heard reports that the Dutch colonial government hadn't pacified the Asmat as much as they were saying, that the head-hunting raids were pretty much in full force.

But at that time he dismissed his own foreboding: maybe he was only stinging from Stephen's dismissal of him over the skull. Maybe he was just hurt that Stephen could replace him so easily with Van Gropius, and wanted to believe that the trip was ill conceived and would be a disappointment. In any case, he was too hurt to interfere. Well, Nightingale thought, ready or not, the boy-king is on his own.

THAT NIGHT THE HOUSE WAS QUIET. EACH MAN WAS INTENT ON organizing his work, his possessions, his thoughts. How strange to imagine that this dream of the mountains was about to end. As the hours passed, the silence between the five of them became funereal. Stephen walked out onto the airfield wearing two sweaters and a knit cap against the cold. He was upset by the interaction with Nightingale. He knew that it was his fault, that he'd erected the wall between them without really meaning to. He liked John so much. But at that moment it seemed like too much to figure out, to make it right between them.

Stephen sat down at the edge of the airfield and looked out at the amphitheater of mountains. In the distance he could see woodsmoke rising lazily into the air, gray on blue. I hope, he thought, that this is what heaven looks like.

Soon a soft wind blew him away and only the mountains were left, vast and still, gazing down on the moonlit valley and its villages below.

# 9

## THE VISIT

IT TOOK STEPHEN THREE DAYS TO FLY FROM HOLLANDIA to New York City. By the time he got home, he was more tired than he'd ever been in his whole life. Back at 1062 Park Avenue he slept through the days and at two A.M. was fully awake. He wandered through the empty rooms that were full of the familiar smell of home: of dried lavender, must, lemon oil and cigarette smoke. Nothing felt real yet. The life he had lived in this apartment, he thought, could have been anybody's.

He was glad to be alone. Marguerite was in England with her cousins, and his father was up in Albany. He emptied all his clothes and books from his luggage onto the floor and lay in bed looking at them as he drifted in and out of sleep.

Stephen had spent most of his trip from New Guinea lost in thought, planning his voyage back to the Asmat. And he'd decided to visit Sheila. One last try. If she wouldn't love him now, he would be able to accept it, he thought; he'd go off to the Asmat and forget her.

ON MONDAY STEPHEN CAUGHT THE MORNING FERRY TO FIRE Island. The Atlantic was green and choppy under the old, loud boat. He looked out at the water, at the Long Island coast retreating through the early-morning haze, and opened his mouth to taste the salt spray and breathe the fishy smell of the ocean into his lungs.

His rucksack (that still smelled of Koa woodsmoke) was bulging with cheese, bread, bottles of Bordeaux wrapped in pages of *The New York Times*, chocolates and his own books and pencils and sketchbook, as though re-entering the past were only a matter of diligently assembling its ornaments and then re-enacting its movements. In all love there is some madness, but in all madness there is some reason. Isn't that how the quote went? Stephen shook his head. The Atlantic distracted him. The sea was so moody that day.

The wind blowing in from the ocean across the narrow island, through the pines along the dunes and onto his skin, had a memory of ice in it, a bite of true northern cold. He walked slowly, breathing it all in, feeling a tame faraway sun just beginning to glow through the clouds. He got off the boardwalk and stood on the sand watching the waves get whipped into whitecaps out at sea and then crash onto the steep beach, one following the other, as though they were after something. He had missed the sea when he was in the Highlands. He loved it, this breeze, the salty green stretching out to meet the horizon.

STEPHEN SAW SHEILA BEFORE SHE SAW HIM. SHE WAS INSIDE HER
house, sitting next to the woodstove, reading, her hair wrapped
up in a turquoise-colored scarf, wearing a black sweater and
pants, her bare feet resting on the floor. She looked up from her
book and saw him through the window.

He walked onto the deck and slid open the glass door. Sheila
didn't move; she only watched him.

"Stephen Hesse, I presume?" she said.

"It's me."

She nodded and smiled and sat there without saying anything. Then: "I'm moving to Paris with Jean next month."

Stephen was dumbstruck. Hot shame and disappointment
flowed through him.

"Should I leave?" he asked, feeling absurd standing there, so
eager to see her, his rucksack strapped onto his back and with his
new short, scruffy beard. Why was he doing this to himself?
Why, when he knew, he *knew* that she didn't want him?

"No," she said, closing the book in her lap. "I just thought I
should tell you."

She was as full and rich as his memory of her. But actually
seeing her unnerved him. He looked at her mouth, her long fingers, with their short fingernails painted red. She was feline, like
a sleepy lioness, alert under hooded eyes.

"Where is Jean?" he asked.

"I don't know," she said. "He could still be on his buying trip
in France or he might be back on West Eleventh Street by now,"
she said. "You're as brown as a coconut, Stephen. I liked your
letters very much. You know, you really do write beautifully."

Everything she said was delivered in the same cool, flat way, but her flattery brought the blood back to his brain. He took off his rucksack and sat down on a sun-bleached, falling-apart rattan chair by the door.

"Have you thought more about writing a book?" she asked.

Stephen shook his head, no. He still couldn't speak. The wind knocked against the house and rushed flurries of sand across her deck. His mind blinked as he looked around absently, noting what had changed, what was the same. He saw that her new paintings leaning up against the wall were lovely: a series of tiny canvases with green, yellow, and gray washes. But looking at them was painful; they were yet another thing off-limits to him now.

"Have you been much off the island since March?" he asked.

"Yeah," she answered, watching him with her dark yellow-green lion eyes.

She wasn't asking him to leave. She wasn't angry. He could stay and talk to her for a while.

Stephen stood up, walked into the kitchen and unpacked the rucksack, lining up the cheese, the loaf of pumpernickel, the mortadella, the chocolates, the bottles of wine, along the counter.

Sheila followed him and opened the wine and made omelets for them. They ate the chocolate and cheddar that he had brought. Everything tasted good. The rhythm of the waves crashing in the distance and the wind and the wine relaxed his upset a little. But in the back of his mind, the fact that they still hadn't touched each other, not even a brush of fingertips, buzzed like a mosquito. Why *wasn't* she sending him away? Or was she?

HE TOLD HER ABOUT THE HIGHLANDS, ABOUT EBABOME AND Nightingale, as if he were telling her a story about someone else.

As he went on, he realized how much of him was in his story, and that he could finally see all of it because she was there listening: what he wanted to do, what he had done. He felt it twice as much, telling her; and the frightening, upsetting parts of his trip to the Highlands became coated in the vision of it that he poured out for her. She saw the further, higher goal, the place he really wanted to go, what he wanted to accomplish. Her attention, her admiration, was narcotic.

Even though Stephen had slipped into the different, better, sphere of existence that held out the possibility of achievement and happiness that he always experienced when he was with her, now there was a new sensation mingled in, unpleasant and cold. What was this new pose she had struck with him—sisterly? motherly? He felt sick from the distance she had spread between them. He couldn't believe that she loved Jean; he wouldn't even believe that Jean existed.

He kissed her, and when she kissed him back, without resistance or ardor, it was like she was pressing down on a bruise.

"Are you *really* going away with Jean?" he breathed in her ear.

"Oh yes, Stephen," she said softly. "And you must understand that I'm not going to leave him."

She was so close to him. He took her all in: her hair, her neck, her arms, her beautiful mouth. He knew he should leave, that he should spare himself what was to come. But instead he walked outside onto the deck and stretched his arms wide, stood on his toes and felt the sun, the waves in the distance, the smell of pine trees and the drying wood of the boardwalk. The sky was too blue. It was a sky of the Northern Hemisphere: yellow sun, white puffy, elongated clouds. He turned and looked at Sheila through the glass doors, standing at her sink, washing their lunch dishes.

He watched her hands covered in soap, the abstracted look on her face. It was like staring at a painting: the white house, her black sweater with its sleeves pushed up to her elbows, the intense aqua-blue of her head scarf. Jealousy and distress and sexual desire swirled around in him.

He went back inside and she turned and smiled at him. He felt her wordless, gentle resistance. There was nothing else to say. She didn't want him there anymore.

He walked over to her and leaned forward and untied her scarf so that her brown-gold hair fell over her shoulders.

"Don't you love me at all anymore?" he asked, swamped in self-pity, looking into her eyes.

"Stephen," she said, smiling up at him but with her same faraway, awful, beatific smile. "Of course I do."

He didn't think that she was even trying to sound convincing. She picked up an opaque white glass jar from the counter and began rubbing thick white cream into her hands. It filled the room with the smell of perfumey roses.

"You know, Stephen. You do remember that I'm eight years older than you?"

"What does that mean?"

She shrugged her shoulders and walked over to her couch and sat down. Stephen's mind was narrowing into a tunnel. The pain he was feeling was worse than physical pain. He followed her to the couch and sat in front of her, on his knees.

"Jesus, Sheila. What can I do? What would make you change your heart? If you ask me to stay, I'll stay. I'll never go back to

New Guinea, I'll never go anywhere without you again. We can go to Europe. If you want, we can buy a house there."

"Why on earth should I ask you to stay here, or quit going to New Guinea, when I want you to go and travel and live and write? You've already started. C'mon."

But everything she said was ashes in his mouth. He didn't want his life. He wanted her. He was thinking that this was the only woman, the only person, who had ever truly seen him, who could ever truly see him. And now it was going to stop.

"Don't send me away." He put his face in his palms. "I can't, Sheila. Please don't send me away." And then he was crying.

"Please. Please. Please. Stephen. Don't be ridiculous."

Hot tears poured down Stephen's cheeks. He saw so painfully clearly what he was doing—embarrassing himself, looking like a desperate, hysterical fool. But he couldn't control it. Right then, he was no more than his feelings.

"I love you so much, Sheila."

"Oh, Stephen. I am sorry about all of this. I don't know what to say."

He stayed sitting on his knees, tears falling. She wouldn't relent. He knew that he was only making the separation between them more defined, but he couldn't stop. Her face, her body, her smell, was all that he could think of. The idea of being banished from her forever was terrifying. Or even if he could see her, he would not be allowed to touch her or kiss her. He could not imagine it.

"Stephen," Sheila said, frowning but full of a strained impersonal kindness, like a nurse. "Won't you please stand up, sweetheart?"

But he couldn't. His desperation, his nervous tension, the ache in his chest, kept him on the floor, unable to regain his equilibrium. Instead of standing up, without knowing what he was doing, he pressed his forehead to the ground and spread out his arms to her, like a Muslim prostrate in prayer.

The worst thing was that he saw everything so clearly. Some lonesome part of his mind was observing, detached as a movie camera. The fading light, the waves lapping at the beach, the wind. He saw himself on the floor, pathetic, a laughable thing. Sheila stood up from the couch, went into the kitchen, got a cigarette and lit it. She looked at him and then glanced out the window. How could she reject him when he really, *really* wanted her? More than anything he'd ever wanted?

And Sheila herself was wondering the same thing. She hadn't meant to become so thoroughly uninterested in Stephen—it had just happened, like a door swinging shut. He was a child to her, not an erotic being, although his desire, the strength of his feeling, still moved her. But while he was away, she had realized that he didn't hold her at all and that she must break with him. That she must make it clean and final.

At the same time, she still recognized how remarkable he was. She felt sorry for him and guilty for this heartache. When she looked at him, it made her so sorry to think that he might never achieve what was inside him. His money, his name, his family were such a dark curse.

She saw him fluttering around her, the pain, the genuine feeling, and it didn't evoke matching passion in her, only sadness. He *was* beautiful-looking. And she meant what she had said about his writing. She had no doubt that if he hadn't been born a Hesse, he could have become an important writer.

No matter how difficult the compromise she had with Jean, it was what she wanted. At least she thought she did. Stephen drained her, like a child would. He was so arrogant, too—showing up unannounced whenever he felt like it, insisting that she be present and pay attention to him. Unknowingly, she thought, he treated her like a high-end servant. She *must*, she *had* to. But still, she hadn't guessed how upset he would be.

She went back to the couch and sat down next to him and stroked her fingers through the soft, grown-out curls that dangled down to his shoulders, fine like a young girl's hair, dark and soft.

He looked up at her.

"What about marrying me? Would you marry me?"

"*Marry* you?" she echoed.

"Why not? You know I love you, Sheila. I thought about you the whole time I was away. I looked forward to seeing you, to being with you, so much."

"Marriage. Stephen, no. No, darling, no." But her mind was on fire at the thought of it. She couldn't help it—Stephen's money leered at her, seductive, carnal. The sheer enormity of the Hesse millions pulled at her with all their power. He was offering her a chance to live another life, to enter a new skin. A chance to dwell among the titans who owned the earth.

"Marriage—it's—no," she said. "My God, Stephen. I'm not the person for you to marry."

It had never occurred to her that he would ask her to marry him. No one ever had, not even Jean. Her house, Stephen's hair under her fingers—it all slipped away as she got lost in thought. But after all, her will was as clear as a boulder in the middle of a river. She didn't want to give away that much of her life; she didn't want the demand. She was afraid of her own greed for things, for beautiful things, of the pretzel she would need to twist herself into to marry Stephen Hesse. No.

She had her own small income, her painting, her house by the sea. Even if she never broke into the art world, she still wanted to paint; she still wanted her solitude. She had Jean, who roused her sexually, who had always roused her sexually, as Stephen, she knew, never would.

Stephen stared at her, flushed, his eyes wet with tears.

"Darling, no," she said. "No, we aren't going to get married. But aren't you something for asking me."

"Aren't I something?" he said quietly.

Sheila felt stupid and blind, as though she were fumbling in a dark room, knocking things off shelves. Stephen was holding his face in his hands. What was she doing? She couldn't believe what was unfolding. Some remote, unknown part of her psyche was shielding her from her impulse to give in, to stopper Stephen's grief, to plunge, frenzied and greedy, into the sea of Hesse oil.

However, looking at him right then she felt so bad and so guilty that she wavered. Perhaps she could be with him for a while, until he got older and his feeling for her eased in its intensity. He was generous—she would be a rich woman. But still her will rebelled against it. The idea of marrying him seemed like a kind of imprisonment. The bird in the golden cage. No. She wouldn't do it. One day Stephen would be the age she was now, and he'd understand that time and chance happen to everyone and that these emotions that felt as real to him as the house he was sitting in were not material. She truly believed that.

She imagined that as he got older, the depth of his thought could grow until it was dazzling, that his reconciliation with who he was, his family, his name, would happen and that this early-fall day on Fire Island, all of it, would be a flutter of a memory in his heart. And she would brag that once upon a time a prince of America had begged her to marry him. Already, tiny bubbles were popping in her mind at the thought of it—a Hesse had dropped to his knees and asked her to marry him. Because that was all she saw him as now, a Hesse.

SHEILA SAT WITH STEPHEN ON THE COUCH. SHE SMOKED WHILE he sat there staring into her kitchen, silent.

"I'll make you a drink," she said, and made them both gin and tonics. "Are you feeling better?" she asked after a while.

"I'm feeling great," Stephen said.

He was looking down at the floor so that he didn't have to see her face.

"You've missed the evening ferry, you know. They only run two a day in the off-season," she said.

"What?" he said. "Now what?"

"You'll stay here. I'll get you a blanket."

It was dark out. Stephen hadn't been aware of the day passing.

Sheila spread a blanket out on the couch. "I'll see you in the morning."

She was gone then, lost into her bedroom. Stephen stared at a piece of driftwood propped against the wall. He was completely worn-out. There wasn't a drop of life in him. Soon, though, the particular human smell of Sheila's house agitated him. He couldn't be under her roof, breathing in her essence for hour upon endless hour. He walked out onto the deck and spent the night there, wrapped in her blanket, cold, too alert to fall asleep, his gaze fixed on the same patch of boardwalk and sand and beach grass. At dawn he got his rucksack and walked to the dock to wait for the first ferry.

STEPHEN WAS UNABLE TO SLEEP THROUGH THE NIGHT FOR THE TWO weeks he was in New York getting ready to leave for the Asmat. Even when he went up to Cambridge to meet with Professor Adams, driving eighty miles an hour through Connecticut and Massachusetts, he was as upset as the night he had lain awake on Sheila's deck.

Won't it ever leave me? he wondered as he wandered through the Harvard campus, which looked gray and sorry. Why couldn't he call up one happy memory of this place? And why should she, of all the people in the world, torture him? It was never-ending, the tightness of his chest, his swollen-up sore throat, his heartache. She was ordinary. She was foolish, pretentious, too studied. She was old. A spinster. Promiscuous. Unpresentable. There were thousands and thousands of women more beautiful than Sheila in Cambridge, in New York. What a mess, he thought.

Professor Adams's office was just as Stephen remembered it, the Persian rugs as beautiful, rich, with their deep, dyed colors, the books and artifacts conveying a sense of the explorer returned. It was the den of a Great Man, in the Victorian sense. But it wasn't a self-conscious space. The office felt natural and gracious, an extension of Adams himself.

Hesse had brought hundreds of photographs of Koa for the professor, including duplicates of the pictures of the village women he had taken for Sheila.

"Wonderful, Stephen," Adams said, and put the unopened box of photos on a shelf behind him.

"Do you want to check them?" Stephen asked.

"No, I'm sure they're right. I'll look them over this evening."

Stephen nodded, upset at Adams's indifference to the photographs, to him.

"John Nightingale tells me you're going to the coast, to the Asmat."

"Yes. I'm leaving in a week and a half."

"Aha. I've never been there. Supposed to be incredible."

"I hope so."

"Aren't you going to be getting there right at the start of the rainy season?"

"No, not really. Erich says we'll have a good month before the monsoon starts."

"Ah, I see."

"Listen. Professor Adams, I had a hell of a time in Koa. I wanted to thank you for including me on the expedition."

"Not at all. You were a tremendous help. It wouldn't have been the same without you." And then: "Are you still planning to start graduate work next year?"

"I'm not sure. Do you think I should?" Stephen asked tentatively.

"I think that's entirely up to you."

Professor Adams smiled, but it felt like a smirk to Stephen.

"So what you're saying is that you don't think it'd be a great tragedy for modern anthropology to lose me?"

Professor Adams started and looked into Stephen's eyes. He shook his head.

"That's not it at all. That's not what I meant at all." Professor Adams was frowning.

"Isn't it? Well, I'm glad to hear that." Stephen seemed close to tears.

Unexpectedly, all of the ugly, difficult feelings that Adams had held about Stephen when they were in the field surfaced into the room. There was no way for the professor to gather them up, like a bag of spilled marbles, and hide them away.

Professor Adams seemed lost. He opened his mouth to speak and then shut it. After a few moments Stephen turned around and left Professor Adams in his perfect office.

THE FOLLOWING WEEK GOVERNOR HESSE CAME DOWN TO THE city from Albany.

Stephen had spent three days preparing for his father's visit. He worked in the darkroom at the Hesse Museum for hours, developing prints from his Koa negatives. The rainforest, women soaking strips of banana leafs at the brine pools, Ebabome's funeral, a line of warriors in full battle gear, children playing at the edge of the airfield. He drew detailed maps of Netherlands New Guinea and eastern British New Guinea, the Koa Valley, the long fingerlings of the Asmat River's tributaries.

He bought catalogs of Asmat carvings from Dutch museums and typed up a list of ideas for exhibiting the type of artwork he hoped to bring back with him before the New Year. He wanted to come back with so much Asmat art that eventually he would be able to mount a show that presented a complete picture of primitive life. It was a Hesse-size ambition, and he knew the idea would please Nicholas.

But as he stood there next to his father gazing down at his

own photographs spread out like a deck of cards, Stephen realized that he wanted something else from the governor—that the whole time he'd been getting ready to see his father, the whole time he'd been in the Highlands, he'd been expecting something from Nicholas Hesse when he got back. Something more than his attention or his interest in New Guinea or in the Harvard expedition. But what *did* he want? What could he want? Even now, he didn't know what it was, only that his desire for it was part of his physical self, like a bad taste on his tongue.

Stephen had never forgiven his father for leaving him to grow up all alone with Marguerite. But that was years ago, ancient history, and who can fix the past? There was nothing Nicholas could do now about whatever happened then. It was over. But still, Stephen thought, he had never had a real father when he was little, when it counted. His fatherlessness had always embarrassed him, as though he had a harelip or a missing limb. Stephen's anger at Nicholas was coiled deep in his belly, a sleeping venomous snake that had been stirred first by Sheila and then by the trip up to Harvard. A flash of pure rage surged through his blood.

"Do you want to have lunch?" his father asked.

Stephen didn't answer. He stared at the bright light glowing through the governor's immense wall of windows. New York City spread out into the distance. The office smelled of cleaning fluid and cigarette smoke. Dour Mrs. Lyle hovered. Stephen felt as if his life were caught in a snare. Mrs. Lyle was like Cerberus, peering at them, listening, never allowing any peace or privacy. Why didn't his father send her away?

Nicholas glanced at the clock on the wall.

"Shall we go to lunch?" the governor repeated.

"I'm sorry. I've got a lunch date already," Stephen lied, smiling.

"Oh." His father frowned. "Can't you reschedule? Isn't this
the only chance we have to get together before you leave?"

"I think it is."

"Well, Stephen, how about it then? Can't you change the
date with whoever it is you're seeing?"

"No. I'm really sorry, Father. I can't."

Stephen looked at his father's face, his skin, the thin blond-
gray hair, his black glasses. Stephen had spent the years of his
childhood knowing this face from a single photograph that Marguerite had framed and put in his room. How weird it used to
make him feel staring at the black-and-white image of his father.
In all those years at 1062 Park Avenue, he had only ever
glimpsed Nicholas in the flesh once, rushing into a waiting car.

No, he had been all alone with Marguerite. The only other
people who spent time in the apartment were the servants,
maids and nannies in uniforms, who were kind, mostly, but in a
way weren't really people at all. Stephen had dreamed of escap-
ing his mother's need, which spilled from her like an overflowing
bathtub. But whenever he tried, whenever he stayed late at
school or meandered on his way home through Central Park, sitting on a bench, reading until it was dark, or fantasized about her
death or about running over to his unknown father's apartment
and begging for shelter, he was sorry. (What a hellish temptation
it was all those years that his father, a savior from dark, cloying,
endless Marguerite, was living out his life in the opposite tower
of the same building! On some days Stephen couldn't stand it.
How could Nicholas never call to see him, never check up on
him? In his rage, he had wanted to jump out the window and

feel his body crack into pieces on the sidewalk.) His mind always wandered back to his mother, and although he didn't know it, his attachment to Marguerite was as strong as hers to him.

"So, no lunch, my boy?" Nicholas said quietly, interrupting Stephen's thoughts.

"No." Stephen shook his head, flushing. He was still so, so angry.

"You can't know how disappointed I am, Stephen. I was looking forward to it so much."

"I really am sorry."

"How healthy you look," his father said, taking him in. "But you've always been strong, the only true athlete among us. Will you be back for Christmas?"

"I don't know yet."

The governor reached out and took Stephen's hand and held it in between his. It was a funny, intimate gesture and it completely disarmed Stephen. For a split second, a warm current flowed from father to son uninterrupted, and the primitive, unknowing fantasy that his father was *his*—his and his mother's, the trinity of father and mother and son that Stephen couldn't remember but which existed, trapped in time, at the bottom of his soul—rushed through him.

"I really would love to see you for Christmas, Stephen. Up at Haleyville. I want us to talk about the future, about *your* future. Try to make it back in time, won't you?"

The governor let go of Stephen's hand and walked him to the door. A desperate, frightened feeling rose up in Stephen. He didn't want to leave at all. But he knew he couldn't stay. Mrs. Lyle was still standing there, holding a stack of typewritten pages, glancing from father to son with her cool, lizardy stare.

"Well, I guess it's good-bye and good luck then." Nicholas patted his son on the shoulder. "Keep me posted. Let me know if you need anything."

"I will, Father."

The governor smiled, his green eyes far away behind his glasses, his thick hands hanging by his sides. He was going to say something else, and then he didn't. Instead, he vanished. In a flash the governor was gone, trailing behind Mrs. Lyle, hidden forever behind his door.

Stephen stood there for a few moments staring at the closed door, lost in feeling, in garbled memories and thoughts. But soon the governor's staff, the outer office, bulged into his consciousness, the *click-clack-ping* of a dozen typewriters, the smell of cigarette smoke and telephones jingling: the sounds of the state government heaving itself forward. Stephen took the elevator down to the lobby and walked out into the swirling city.

THE NEXT MORNING, STEPHEN WOKE UP EARLY. HE RODE HIS bicycle through Central Park as the sun rose and turned the world light blue and then gray with a pink halo. He could feel the day rolling into the city. The air was still and cool; the park's damp earth-and-grass smell filled his nose. Unthinking, he cycled down Second Avenue, dodging taxicabs as the East Side woke up, the honking, the smell of gasoline and brewing coffee drifting over him. He rode farther downtown and then across Fourteenth Street until he was in the West Village, which was still slumbering.

He stopped in front of Sheila's apartment house. Her window was open, the spinning black rubber leaves of a fan visible. The fire escape was full of plants, their dark green leaves dripping over terra-cotta pots, entangled with the black-painted iron bars. He knew Jean was in there, awake with jet lag. Maybe reading the paper, drinking a coffee. Maybe packing for Fire Island. Stephen turned his bike around and rode back uptown.

STEPHEN'S FLIGHT TO LOS ANGELES LEFT IDLEWILD AT SIX O'CLOCK in the morning. A fantasy of Sheila looped through his mind as he sat in the back of the taxicab, on the way to Queens: she would be at the airport, waiting for him. She would show up unexpectedly to see him off. In his fantasy, she told him that they'd see about things between them when he returned at Christmas. She'd decided not to go to France with Jean after all. Maybe there *was* hope for the two of them. They would take things as they came.

But of course she wasn't there; he had never told her what day he was leaving, what time his flight took off. No. There were only other travelers at Idlewild, footsteps echoing through the terminal, suitcases, uniforms. Everything was sorted into place; nothing was unexpected. Sheila wasn't in love with him: another simple, unadorned fact.

His plane lifted off, up into the morning, into a clear fall day. For the first time since he'd been back in the Northern Hemisphere, Stephen felt light. New Guinea lay ahead, beckoning him with all of her green beauty. He was impatient then to be back in the wild. To exchange the old world for the new.

The sun gleamed, bouncing off the airplane's silver wings as it rose above the eastern coast of North America, heading west through the clouds into the colorless sky.

# BOOK 3

*In short I have only two possibilities: either I can*

*be like some traveler of the olden days, who was*

*faced with a stupendous spectacle, all, or almost*

*all of which eluded him, or worse still, filled him*

*with scorn and disgust; or I can be a modern*

*traveler, chasing after the vestiges of a vanished*

*reality.*

—CLAUDE LÉVI-STRAUSS, *TRISTES TROPIQUES*

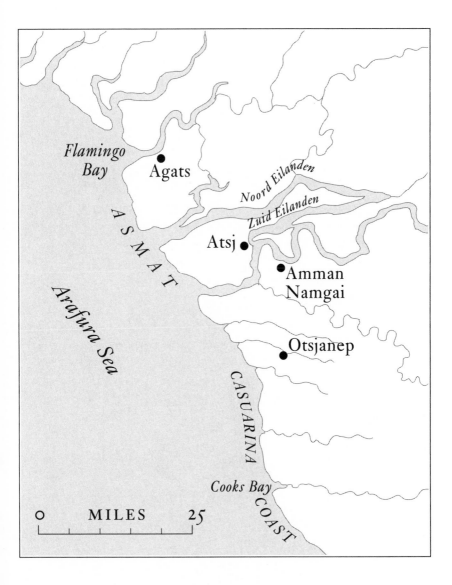

Flamingo
Bay

Agats

*Noord Eilanden*

*Zuid Eilanden*

A S M A T

Atsj

Amman
Namgai

*Arafura Sea*

Otsjanep

CASUARINA

Cooks Bay

COAST

O        MILES        25

# 10

## CAPTAIN COOK IN THE TORRES STRAIT

THE SEAWATER IS GRITTY, COFFEE COLORED AND OPAQUE FROM the mountain runoff. Almost every day bursting-full rivers of rainwater rush down from the mountains, carrying roots and branches and soil through the swampy lowland plains, and then empty out like gushing sewers into the Arafura. The landscape is tone on tone: browns, greens, white, the dirty white of clouds heavy with rain. From the air, the colors along the coast bleed into only two shades: the bluish brown of the sea, the greenish brown of the land. Rain and rain and mud and heat and wet. At low tide, miles of mudflats appear.

Acres of sea grass grow in the silty water along the margin of the Torres Strait. Puffer fish and sea horses swim in the bubbling, oxygen-rich water as crabs and lobsters crawl through a maze of grass stalks. Fat dugongs troll the meadows munching on the tough, fibrous grass and its juicy roots.

The Arafura is immense but shallow, strewn with reefs and tiny, barren islands. It feels like a forgotten place, empty even of its ghosts.

DURING THE LAST GREAT ICE AGE, THE ARAFURA WASN'T A SEA AT all but an arid, lifeless savannah that connected New Guinea to Australia; seedpods from the trees and plants of the massive southern continent drifted north, taking root in the fertile black New Guinean soil, crawling up into the mountains, spreading out along the northern and southern coasts. A few intrepid small animals scurried across the hot, dry land belt, too: rats and marsupials, maybe egg-laying monotremes and primitive, flightless cassowaries. But then, when the glaciers receded, the Arafura flooded. The brine swelled and seeped out to the east through the narrow Torres Strait to meet the Coral Sea and west to the Indian Ocean. Once again New Guinea and the Terra Australis were separated by the sea.

Before the first European explorers ever floated through this part of the Pacific, fleets of Maccassan tribesmen from the Celebes Islands fished the Arafura, harvesting bêches-de-mer, intensely colored sea slugs that ripple through shallow water. The Maccassans dried and cured the bêches-de-mer and sold them as an aphrodisiac, via the ancient Asian markets, to the Chinese.

The Arafura's shoals are full of fish: queen fish, marlin, sailfish, triggerfish, barracuda, sharks, eels. They swim to and fro through the silty seawater, along the channels and ridges that lead to the ledge of the continental shelf and its steep drop down to the deep darkness of the Pacific.

IN 1770 THE BRILLIANT AND FEARLESS ENGLISH MARINER CAPTAIN
James Cook sailed his ship, *Endeavour,* into the Arafura Sea.
The shallow sea and its eighty-mile-wide, hazardous strait had
been kept a secret in Europe for nearly 150 years. Luis Vaez de
Torres, working for the Spanish government, discovered the
narrow passage in 1604, the year after ambitious, greedy Queen
Elizabeth I died. The body of water and the priceless trade route
it afforded had been fiercely guarded information by the Spanish, and so Cook, when he arrived in the Arafura, was on a second, covert, part of a scientific journey to the South Pacific. He
was following top-secret British instructions, given to him
sealed, to sail south as far as 40 degrees latitude to determine
whether the mythic continent of Australia existed, or was there
only endless ocean in that unexplored part of the world?

By the time Cook got to the Arafura, he had long ago found
Terra Australis Incognita; in fact *Endeavour* had almost wrecked
on the Great Barrier Reef. Her crew had spent the last six weeks
fixing her, living on a little patch of coastal Queensland, in a
place today called Cooktown. The *Endeavour's* crew took off in
their patched up, leaking ship ("the most dangerous navigation
that perhaps ship was ever in," Cook would later write), sailing
into the remote, uncharted Arafura. The *Endeavour,* a sturdy
boat, originally built as coal-carrying ship, stayed close to land,
within visual distance of the New Guinea coast. But Cook's
sailors were frightened away from landing to gather fresh water
and fruit by a battle formation of Asmat warriors, who paddled
out to meet them in a massive brigade of long, narrow canoes.

The Asmat were fierce, head-hunting tribesmen, resplendent in feather crowns and war paint, chanting an intimidating, rhythmic song as they dug their paddles into the Arafura. Traditionally, before battle, the Asmat threw handfuls of lime dust at their enemies to disorient them. The panicked British seamen mistook the clouds of lime dust for gunpowder and kept sailing west, leaving the Asmat to themselves.

CAPTAIN COOK KEPT THE COURSE, DUE WEST, TOWARD THE Indonesian archipelago. But *Endeavour* would not leave the Arafura's treacherous currents easily. The ship suffered another near wreck in its shallows. Cook's crew sailed the ailing, leaking, water-heavy *Endeavour* to Jakarta. After two months in Jakarta, the boat was fixed. As they set off for home, Captain Cook prepared his report: besides charting the eastern coast of Australia and most of New Zealand, he had navigated the murky, hazardous Arafura. He had found a new sea route for the mighty British empire and her fleet.

Cook's knowledge was with him, in his quarters, like a wild animal stowed in a canvas sack—alive, wondrous, frightening, barely containable. They sailed the wounded *Endeavour* back to England slowly and carefully.

> Oh! dream of joy! is this indeed
> The lighthouse top I see?
> Is this the hill? Is this the kirk?
> Is this mine own countree?

The *Endeavour* didn't get back to England until July 1771, and then Cook's knowledge, his discoveries, escaped and flew over the British Isles to Europe and Russia, to the colonies across the Atlantic. Cook's news—that, after all, the world was limitless—lush, without end—was unstoppable.

# 11

## *HUIS TE KOOP*

IT WAS HOT EVEN BEFORE DAWN ARRIVED. STEPHEN SAT ON THE porch of Father Dougherty's house breathing in thick, wet air that was full of mud and the sea. He sipped lukewarm Nescafé, thinking about home and about New Guinea, letting his mind wander as he watched the only other souls out-of-doors in Irma village, two little boys squatting on the riverbank. The children were completely engrossed in each other, skinny arms and legs entwined, talking, giggling, whispering; grooming each other's hair, squashing blood-fat lice between their thumbnails.

Stephen wrote the scene as he watched it, trying to imprint it in his mind. He wanted to put the two boys in the letter he had started for his father, a letter that was already twenty pages long. There, in the Asmat, whenever he thought about the last time he'd seen Nicholas, he winced with embarrassment. He couldn't bear the memory of that visit to his father's office. And so he'd begun writing him a sort of apology, a travel log. He wrote as intimately as he knew how to and saved the best things for his letter, collecting moments like this one, of orange dawn flushing the sky as the boys played on the riverbank.

Stephen had started writing the morning after he arrived in the Asmat, when he was still jet-lagged and heavy with the heat. But as he reread his pages, he thought that, really, this was the letter he would write to Sheila if he could think about her without feeling sick. Or maybe it wasn't for either of them. Maybe these pages were what she had suggested—notes for a book he would write.

He started with his first sight of the swampy, mangrove-snarled Casuarina Coast, wrote it all out like a scene from a movie, like a camera sweeping the landscape in a single, long shot: the blanket of hot, moist air that sat over endless mud plain and jungle, the foaming, dark sea, the winding gray rivers that crawled up into the salt swamps. The hamlets of square, thatch-roofed huts built up on stilts. The oozing, brackish mud that was forever flooded by the backwash of the tides.

There was no coastline, no distinction between the mud below and the sky above and the seawater that stretched out as far as the eye could see. He described the dark, naked men who lived there, who wore crowns of cockatoo feathers and decorated human skulls strung on twine as amulets.

He wrote about the young men who wore necklaces of human vertebrae—their mother's or a favorite maternal aunt's backbones—and strapped delicately carved human bone daggers around their upper arms. Keeping all of it so close, the mortal remains of both their beloved and the enemy they killed, was meant to protect them from their ghosts. The Asmat, Stephen explained to his father, lived in terror of angry, vengeful ghosts. They believed the only way to keep the malevolent spirits away was to frighten them with the sight of their own bones; to frighten and shame them with the physical reminders of the breathing, living creatures they once were.

*Only five years ago,* Stephen wrote in his letter, *almost the whole region was head-hunting. And the skulls go everywhere with their owners—into the jungle, fishing. They touch the bone so often that it develops a sheen and, after a while, starts to look like antique, carved ivory.*

WHAT HE DIDN'T DISCUSS IN THE LETTER WAS HIS EXPERIENCE OF being alone—truly alone—for the first time in his life. Van Gropius acted toward him with the unconscious hostility and reticence of a servant. There was no Adams or Nightingale to interpret or dilute the world around him; no two-way radio hooked up to a network of missionaries and Dutch colonial officers. In the Highlands the other white men, even Nightingale, had kept him within his own borders. But here he was slipping out of himself. Every single moment in the Asmat was his. He was finding out, he thought, what it was to be uncertain, to exist in mystery and not reach for the technology and order of the West. He had complete freedom. No one was watching.

IN THE MIDDLE OF OCTOBER, HESSE HAD MET VAN GROPIUS IN Hollandia, the capital of Netherlands New Guinea, with its oversize airstrip and town of quaint pastel-painted wood houses lined up along unpaved streets. Hollandia felt like a summer home in the midst of being shut up for the season, still echoing with the lives that had just left. Van Gropius pointed out the signs all over the capital; HUIS TE KOOP ("house for sale" in Dutch) was tacked on fences and front doors.

"We have given up. The Dutch may as well give the keys to the Indonesians," Van Gropius said gloomily. "There's nothing here anymore. Not for a Dutchman."

"Surely it's not all over," Stephen said. "Aren't you being dire?"

"There is nothing here for a white man," Van Gropius said, "nothing but to pick at the bones."

THE TWO OF THEM FLEW FROM HOLLANDIA IN A LOUD, BOUNCING DC-3 left over from the war to the southern coast, to Merauke, and then raced to catch a steamboat, the first one in months, headed north for the Asmat town of Agats. Hesse and Van Gropius stayed a few days in the government town, catching their breath and sorting out supplies. Agats was only a few rows of huts on stilts, connected to each other by a boardwalk and filled with mosquitoes, rats, mice, government officials, missionaries, a few anthropologists and New Guineans. Hesse and Van Gropius stayed in the Government Rest House, a small, empty hut with an Asmat-style hearth on the floor.

All the Europeans in Agats (even the nuns who brought stacked pots of steaming rice and curried catfish to the Rest House at lunchtime) wanted to talk about was the coming monsoon and whether the Indonesians would kick all the whites out of the country. The twin calamities—the Indonesians and the seasonal rains—loomed over the place, an opaque cloud of worry that shut out the sun's light but not its infernal heat.

Stephen felt removed from it all, contemptuous of the whites in Agats. If it was time to move, why not move? Why not go back home, or somewhere else, instead of all this cowering like mice waiting for the cat to pounce? He did not see the grave injustice. It wasn't a war, he thought; they weren't being forced to leave Amsterdam.

Hesse and Van Gropius took off from Agats, loaded down with supplies for their trip into the interior. They motored west out into Flamingo Bay and then north, upriver, accompanied by languid crocodiles and thousands of sparrows that twittered at them from the shore. Nipa palms and mangroves lined the river's edge, and tall, spindly trees leaned over, dipping their leaf tips into the gray water.

Stephen began sweating; soon his clothes were as wet as if he had dived into the river. He breathed the air deep into his lungs. He was happy in an entirely new way. His only worry was that the feeling would pass through him before he could catch it and write it down.

Finally, they arrived at Irma village, the first stop Van Gropius had arranged for their art-buying expedition. A Catholic mission sat on the village's riverbank: a rectangular thatch-roof hut built up on stilts with a massive white-painted cross nailed to its beams, so that the giant, silent Christian eye watched all the traffic on the river—the Dutch patrols, the long, narrow dugout canoes the Asmat paddled to go fishing or traveling to marriage and mourning feasts.

Irma village itself sat on a mud floor cut out of the swampy, flat jungle. A swarm of village children, naked and splattered with mud, hooted as Stephen and Van Gropius arrived, running back and forth along the shore, in circles around the priest, who stood waiting to greet them, still and quiet.

STEPHEN WROTE PAGE AFTER BLUE-INKED PAGE TO HIS FATHER about his host in Irma, Father Michael Dougherty. Strange, remote Father Dougherty, who had run this mission since 1958, a small middle-aged man, born in faraway Minnesota, with his rounded belly, short limbs and red hair streaked with pure, sun-bleached white. The priest looked pink and elfin, his face lined by the tropical sun, standing in a brown cassock against the gray mud and endless brown-green blur of the Asmat. Stephen was always aware of his clear, almost colorless light blue eyes and his mouth, surrounded by a white beard, pink lips opening into his red, dark mouth as he ate, as he laughed, as he chatted with his naked Asmat flock in the full heat of the day.

At the beginning of their stay, Stephen was bewitched by Father Dougherty, as though he and Van Gropius had stumbled upon a druid from an Arthurian tale. The priest knew everything, it seemed, about the place and her people. Father Dougherty was a scholar of Irma village; he had ring binders full of typed-up notes inside the mission and the deep, restrained calm of a monk. Father Dougherty didn't mention the Indonesians, the Dutch or the monsoon. He was the kind of man, Stephen thought, who would stay here, or wherever he thought he should be, no matter what storms raged at him.

At night Father Dougherty dutifully, generously taught Stephen about the region, explaining customs, alliances, taboos, while Van Gropius read in his sleeping bag under mosquito netting.

But the priest didn't invite his guests to mass or to come along when he visited the sick or taught his English class. Soon Stephen understood: Father Dougherty didn't want them too near.

*And fair enough,* Stephen wrote, stung by the priest's rejection, *since the anthropologist and the missionary are eternal antagonists—like two men courting the same woman.*

Stephen wandered alone through Irma as the Asmat days unfolded and wilted and finally curled up into evening. They had to stay longer than they had planned. Van Gropius was sick with fever and diarrhea, so he napped during the heat of the day and sipped cooled boiled water under his netting. Stephen dug out his Leica and started photographing: the silhouette of stilted huts against the river, children playing, chasing one another in the mud, the small fleets of canoes full of women and fishing nets as the men paddled downriver to the sea in the morning and returned at dusk loaded with tiny shrimp and piles of dying catfish.

In the afternoons he hovered at the men's house, a long rectangular structure in the middle of the village, built up on stilts, thatch-roofed, surrounded by a wide porch. The men who carved wood into the artifacts that Stephen was quietly buying spent their days gathered on the porch, whittling, singing, smoking and gossiping, occasionally curling up on their sides and falling asleep on human-skull headrests. Stephen took photograph after photograph of the sight—a live, sleeping man resting on a skull. The image seemed perfect to him; somehow, all of humanity was bound up in it. Father Dougherty had explained to him that the skulls with their jaws intact belonged to beloved ancestors and the ones with the jaws ripped off were trophies from head-hunting raids. *The men catnap,* he wrote in his notebook, *on skulls with intact jaws.*

Soon the sight of the skulls no longer jolted him. There were so many and they were everywhere. Slowly, the human bones, the mud and smoke smell of the village, the heat, the sound of the language, penetrated his skin and reached his psyche; he felt this place more than the Highlands, more than any place he'd ever been, except for his childhood summers in Maine.

One morning he ventured inside the Irma men's house and discovered hidden in the smoky darkness, at the far end, fourteen skulls, jaws intact, hanging down from the rafters on twine ropes, softly knocking into one another, making a faint *click-click* in the draft. A man was sitting back there with the skulls, smoking tobacco from a bamboo pipe. He looked up at Stephen and then, uninterested, turned back to the slow-burning fire in the hearth.

Stephen wrote in his notebook:

*The difference between our feelings for human remains and the Asmats' is a very simple one. Our feelings seem to be the exact opposite to theirs—so really, in a way, our two cultures actually feel identically about death. Or, at least it seems to me that our two cultures are children of the same parents. We, in the West, are repulsed by and afraid of death and so we hide its evidence—we bury bodies deep in the earth or we burn them up, whereas the people here are repulsed by and afraid of death, too, but instead they keep human bones and skulls with them; on their bodies, in their houses.*

At night, Stephen's mind overflowed with the residue of the day: with the skulls and blood, the villagers, the carvings. Father Dougherty. Lying awake, hot, under his mosquito netting, listening to the mice scamper along the walls, he felt the enormity of where he was. In the early morning, Stephen wandered down to the river to watch its slow, murky flow. If he could see all of this from the right vantage, he thought, he had a chance to understand life.

*It is so unexpected,* he wrote underneath an ink drawing of a carved canoe prow, *but I have found a place where I am completely at ease.*

At first, Stephen was awkward at the men's house. He sat on the porch uninvited, muscling through his own shyness, bringing small gifts of braided, spiced tobacco for the carvers. After a few moments of watching, he would move to an empty stretch of the woven-bamboo floor and drink in the smell of the sun-warmed mud, of the woodsmoke, the tobacco, the musky, dusty smell of the men's house.

He smiled to himself about his porch-sitting. He was like one of the mangy hunting dogs that skulked around: tolerated, allowed to scrounge for scraps. While he was there, he photographed the curlicue designs—praying mantis, pig tusks—carved on the shields then rubbed white with limestone powder, red with hematite, black with soot. He photographed the artists' hands at work, dark fingers entangled in wood, scraping, rubbing, whittling, as they produced one sculpted thing after another.

The pieces were intended for religious ceremonies, Father Dougherty had explained to him; the carvings were a code that the living used to speak to their dead. Stephen recalled the ornate medieval reliquaries his grandfather had collected. Weren't they created from a similar impulse? But he thought the Asmat work was more exciting, less self-conscious, than the medieval European devotional art.

Stephen couldn't believe the power of the Asmat carving. It was as though he'd never seen art before, he thought, never felt it. The sculpture was so aggressive, full of life, perfectly conveying grief and anger, beauty and sex.

"Isn't it amazing?" he'd demand of the recovering Van Gropius. "Isn't this stuff unbelievable? It's unbelievable!"

The Dutchman nodded and agreed; the Asmat made spectacular art, and Stephen hadn't even seen the *bisj* poles yet.

Yet at night, as he cataloged the growing mound of work he was buying, Stephen fretted. He imagined getting back to New York, prying open the crates and revealing container after container of carefully wrapped, ugly, valueless sculpture in front of his father. How could he know if any of it was *really* good? Maybe, he worried, he was affected by the place, by the heat, by his bloated feelings. He didn't trust Van Gropius to tell him whether something was truly good or not. Perhaps this art would lose all its intensity when it was removed from its setting. Having real taste, Nicholas had once said to him, seeing a piece of art and knowing what it is without having to be told, well, his father had said, it's almost as rare as having artistic talent.

IN THE EVENING FATHER DOUGHERTY SERVED HESSE AND VAN Gropius, as he started to feel stronger, tea and tinned curry or corned beef on rice—starchy, salty food, weirdly appetizing, even with its light aftertaste of mud. The priest's hut was built right on the water, and after dark a soft breeze flew in and filled the room with the smell of the river. An unpainted wood cross on the wall was lit up by a kerosene lantern and the flames from the hearth on the floor. Sweet-smelling Chinese bug coils burned constantly.

Father Dougherty had built a small library in one corner: two wood-slab shelves stacked with books that had split spines and wavy, moisture-fat pages. The priest's own Bible, *Argonauts of the Western Pacific*, a first-aid manual, a Malay dictionary, several out-of-date issues of *Time* magazine. His hardbound three-ring binders of field notes carefully labeled—1958, 1959, 1960, 1961. A Smith Corona sat on the table, covered in a plastic apron, pushed aside while they ate. The priest had produced calm in his tiny home, a womb soft with reminders of Western life.

"The Asmat are Papuans, you know," the priest started out that night. "They descend from the tribes that originally settled New Guinea thirty thousand years ago."

It was hard to conceive, even for Father Dougherty, but barely a generation ago the Asmat had had only their physical strength, fire, water, bones and animal teeth as tools to navigate through the world. They had lived a life mostly unchanged for the past thirty millennia.

The head-hunting Asmat had been the most primitive men on earth, but then again, their religion, their art, was as sophisticated as any in the West or the Eastern world, didn't Stephen agree? Yes. Yes. It was undeniable. The magnificence of the carving—in its intricacy, symbolism, its ability to inspire spiritual ecstasy—Father Dougherty said, was, in his opinion, as much a reflection of God's grace as anything Michelangelo had cut out of marble.

But what was so *strange,* so original, so heartbreakingly beautiful, to the priest was that the genius that created Asmat art had not spouted from one man but from generations of men, who had carved anonymously as a sacred, holy act.

"The most famous artwork of the region," Father Dougherty told Stephen, "that hopefully you will get a chance to see on this trip, the *bisj* poles—the Asmat ancestor poles—are carved from mangrove. The work they take! Months of intricate cutting, carv-

ing, scraping, designing—you can't imagine the skill and artistry
required to produce these enormous icons. Well, even the *bisj*
poles aren't meant to last more than eighteen months, much less
an artist's lifetime. After the ritual feast they've been created for is
over, they're of no interest to the community anymore. Can you
imagine—traditionally, the *bisj* are left to rot in the sago swamps!"

Art was part of everyday life; even the creation myth was
centered around carving. Fumeripitj, the first Asmat man, Father Dougherty told them, had drowned in a swamped canoe
and washed up dead on the beach. When a group of magical
birds found him, they were sorry that so lovely and young a man
had died and decided to bring him back to life. But after he was
brought back from the dead, Fumeripitj was lonely, so he carved
men and women out of wood and breathed life into them to
make himself companions. And so came into being the first
Asmat tribes.

"You see," the priest said, "how brilliant it all is? The very
stuff of life is wood. Carving is how you speak to the ancestor-
spirits, and so life and death bleed into each other, in a perfect
spiritual circle."

Stephen watched Father Dougherty float in contemplation.
The pink creases of his face and his white beard, stained yellow
around his mouth from the goose curry, were all that was left of
him.

"But aren't you, you know, I mean, really, aren't all missionaries—aren't you trying to take away all of this and make the
Asmat—really all of New Guinea—Christian?" Stephen asked.

The priest frowned. He emerged from his contemplation,
annoyed. He turned his light blue eyes on Stephen and regarded
him with the blinking, absent glare of a snowy owl.

"I mean, if I understand correctly," Stephen continued, "the Asmats' whole way of life—their art, religion, tribal alliances, kinship structure—all are part of a system that is based on cannibalism and head-hunting. What happens when you take away the age-old beliefs of their culture and replace them with Jesus Christ?"

"Stephen, don't you understand what is really going on around here? You're not on a class trip," the priest said, and glanced at Van Gropius. "Haven't you told him?" he asked, angry and quiet.

Van Gropius shrugged. "Everyone has an idea about New Guinea, Father. The Dutch government, the Catholic and Protestant missionaries, yes? The oil companies. The Indonesians. The Australians. The U.N. Why not the art collectors?"

The priest stared at Van Gropius and shook his head.

"Until very, very recently, the people here, here in Irma—everywhere you'll go on your trip—have been stuck in quicksand, unable to escape from a never-ending nightmare of evil, of head-hunting and cannibalism and black magic. Try to imagine the horror of their day-to-day existence. Always afraid! Terrified of brutal, unspeakable violence, death lurking everywhere. Can you imagine it, Stephen Hesse? I cannot. But I am not, the Catholic Church is *not,* trying to stop the carving or change the Asmat way of life. *On the contrary*—we want to save their culture for them. Except, of course, we cannot, the Dutch and the Indonesians cannot, the *world* cannot, let the head-hunting and cannibalism continue. Or is the art you're buying for your museum in New York City only valuable if these people are eating each other?"

"You are lucky, Stephen," Van Gropius said, interrupting the exchange, turning his back to the priest. "In the whole world, this is the last frontier, the last place that wild men exist. You're getting a taste, a glimpse of it, just as it evaporates, no? Very, very soon the Dutch—the Indonesians maybe?—will put a full stop to the head-hunting." He turned to the priest and said, "And then, perhaps, if all goes well for them, the Asmat will just be poor, peculiar little pretend white men."

Stephen's dinner plate, heaped with rice and goose curry, sat untouched. The priest was so angry; he hadn't expected that. He hadn't meant to provoke him to real anger; he had thought to have a conversation. Every nerve in Stephen's body sensed Father Dougherty's disapproval of him. He knew the priest held the true Christian's antipathy to wealth. A prayer from a poor man's mouth goes straight to God's ear, and isn't it easier for a camel to walk through the eye of a needle than for a rich man to go to heaven? However, Stephen was who he was, born into this mortal coil his father's son. He wanted to be—he thought he deserved to be—loved and forgiven as a child of God as much as anyone else.

"But isn't all this," Stephen said, urged on, hurt by the priest's hostility, "a sort of tragedy? I mean, it seems like the people here doubt the value of their culture, of all the brilliant art they are making. They want *any*thing Western. I mean, y'know, shoelaces, wristwatches, my socks, my hat, *empty cans.*"

"The West is here forever. Nothing will bring back life the way it was before the Europeans arrived, even if you should wish to condemn these folks back to that hell. I am *for* the Asmat people. I want to share God's love. To help them."

Stephen Hesse and the priest stared at each other, both of them just holding back. Van Gropius looked down at his plate and began eating. Eventually, the houseboy, Luke, came and cleared the plates and cutlery. And then there was only the sound of him washing up: dishwater splashing, cutlery scraping against the bottom of the aluminum pan, the fire crackling.

"Well, I *might* be wrong. I'm not pretending I'm on a humanitarian mission, and I know I've only been here a short while. It just seems that the Asmat are being sucked into a world that insists on economic plenty, in our sense—in the Western sense—as the primary ideal," Stephen said at last.

"Gentlemen." Van Gropius stood up from the table, smiling, yawning ostentatiously. "I am too tired to save the Asmat tonight. Good evening."

"Surely, *you* are not suggesting that *I* am teaching these people that 'economic plenty' is any kind of ideal at all!" The priest looked like he was about to start laughing a nasty, mocking laugh.

"But aren't you being just a bit disingenuous, Father Dougherty? Of course you benefit by your association with the West. I mean, is it ethical, really, to convert with the unspoken promise that as Christians these people will be like the white man, with access to endless supplies of wristwatches and outboard motors and braids of *lempeng* tobacco?"

Father Dougherty did not smile. But wasn't it something to be lectured on ethics by Rudolph Hesse's great-grandson! Pitiless, corrupt old Hesse and his evil, bloodstained son. Father Dougherty had been a child during the Fowler Massacre, but it was the epochal event of his youth. All those men and their families killed by the mining company they worked for—his own father weeping ugly, angry tears; the stench of burning gasoline that hung in the air for weeks. It was still so clear in his mind. He had dreamed of it when he found out Stephen would be visiting Irma. The night of the massacre, his mother had opened their door to the miners' wives who'd escaped the bloodshed. Even after all these years, thousands of miles away, Father Dougherty could see those women and their children—covered in filth, bleeding, but so quiet, so weirdly quiet.

No, he didn't care how many millions of dollars the Hesse family gave away to charities, how many libraries and colleges for American Negroes they founded. Their money, this boy's money, was blood-soaked, steeped in the blood of all those coal miners and their families and God knew how many others— weren't the Fowler mines just a tiny portion of their empire?

Father Dougherty's own father had had no choice but to go back to work in the mines after the trouble. Every day he and all the other miners carried the knowledge down into the pit that Rudolph Hesse, the man they were making richer and richer with their bone-grinding labor, had let his guards open fire on hundreds of their brother workers that terrible night, shooting at the striking miners, who were huddled inside canvas tents with their terrified wives and children. And then, when the tent city caught fire, those poor people were left to roast rather than be allowed to join a union.

But this one, the priest thought, Hesse's great-grandson, was something else. As obnoxious and intelligent as you would ex- pect. But there *was* something fine about him, something he hadn't foreseen. Father Dougherty couldn't help himself. He felt for Stephen. For the gate is narrow and the way is hard that leads to life, and those who find it are few. He would pray for this boy.

"And you," Father Dougherty asked quietly, his anger evaporated. He turned his weird blue-white eyes on Stephen. "Are you a Christian?"

"Well. Yes, I am," Stephen said, looking at the priest curiously. "Not a Catholic, though."

"Oh no, no. I know that," Father Dougherty said, nodding his head, smiling a soft, sad smile. "I'm not looking for a convert."

THAT NIGHT, STEPHEN WROTE TO HIS FATHER BY THE LIGHT OF the kerosene lamp about the difficulties of falling asleep in the Asmat. He described the wet heat, the whining, vicious mosquitoes, the constant noise: mice racing over the walls, rats crawling through the thatch roof, the buzz of cicadas, frogs ribbiting, roosters that crowed at midnight and, finally, the predawn earthquakes that rocked him into a few hours of light sleep. While he wrote about the Asmat, a flash of Mount Desert beset him—pine trees in the wind, the sun on the waves, sweet, fragrant roses. He was homesick. The argument with the priest had unsettled him.

He dreamed more than usual that night, vivid, brilliantly colored dreams that bored tunnels through his mind: dreams of the river, fat eels slithering in the mud. He dreamed that Father Dougherty woke him up and led him through the blue night to the men's house. They walked inside and were enveloped in dust and woodsmoke, surrounded by the carvings Stephen had bought: canoe prows, shields, paddles, masks and drums. He could see the fourteen skulls hanging at the back of the house, only now they were tagged with bright-orange FOR SALE signs.

"This is where the two worlds meet, Stephen. The dead and the living meet here," the priest whispered in his ear.

But there were no villagers, no Asmat men, with them—the house was empty of life. Stephen began to feel afraid. Soon he couldn't see from the woodsmoke burning his eyes.

"Where are you?" Stephen whispered. "Are you here, Father Dougherty?"

And then, in his dream, he realized that the priest had left.

# 12

## LUKE

FATHER DOUGHERTY'S MOST SUCCESSFUL CONVERT IN IRMA village was a young man named Biwar Tngene, who had re-named himself Luke after his baptism. Luke Tngene had learned English from the priest. He worked as his houseboy and sang at Sunday mass.

Luke had brown eyes flecked with gold. His skin was a deep red-brown, glistening from the dry-store jasmine-scented oil he rubbed into himself every day. He wore faded pastel cotton shirts and khaki shorts from the boxes of secondhand clothes that Father Dougherty's sister sent from Denver at Christmas-time. Out of the houseboy's earshot, the priest had explained to Hesse and Van Gropius that Luke was from a low-status family. Neither his father nor his maternal uncles had taken heads. Luke's mother's hut sat at the very end of the village, to keep their bad luck from polluting everyone else. Anyway, the priest explained matter-of-factly, no one with any real status would want to be in such close contact with white men.

Luke was a puzzle to Stephen. He was nothing like the passionate young Highlanders he and Nightingale had befriended in Koa. He seemed both stupid and brilliant, obsequious and nasty, although it was true that Luke was the only New Guinean to show any sustained interest in him since he had arrived.

One afternoon Stephen had loaned the houseboy his colored pencils and sketchbook and Luke drew, from memory, dozens of the beautiful, intricate designs that decorate Asmat canoe prows, paddles, shields, drums and the ancestor poles, the *bisj*. He explained every single image as Stephen wrote it all down—symbolism, power, the secret magic they carried—slitting open the sac of his village's beliefs for the young American. He was used to explaining things to Father Dougherty, and Stephen felt how assuredly he did it.

Luke had memorized passages from the Bible, and for the first few days after the art collectors arrived, he quoted them in a booming alto, startling Stephen and Van Gropius as they ate breakfast or tried to organize the chaos of cameras and recording equipment that lay tangled on the priest's floor.

> *Your eye is the lamp of your body!*
> *When your eye is sound, your whole*
> *body is full of light!*

Van Gropius turned to Stephen and whispered, "This whole Christian thing is quite out of hand, no?"

"Rather," Stephen said, and laughed.

"I think the priest and his houseboy are the only two believers for miles, what do you say?"

"Oh," Stephen grinned, "at most."

The evening before Hesse and Van Gropius were to leave Irma village, Luke sat down next to Stephen and watched him sketch a body mask. Stephen had bought it early that morning and he was still engrossed in it. It looked like a monster out of a dream, its head woven out of dried palm leaves, strings of gray Job's-tears seeds as its hair, two painted oval disks for its enormous, frightening eyes and long leaves hanging down as a skirt.

Father Dougherty had explained the woven artifact to Stephen while its owner, a quiet, elderly Asmat, crouched beside it. The body masks were made to represent specific individuals who had recently died. Once or twice a year, the village would have a death feast, like an enormous weeklong wake, and all the masks of the recently dead were welcomed in. Then, the priest explained, the dead and the living could feast together, until finally, at night, the spirits disappeared into the forest and thus the dead were transformed into ancestral beings.

"Ghosts, shades, souls, however you put it," the priest said as Stephen scribbled in his notebook.

Stephen was a meticulous draftsman. He drew slowly, cross-hatching, shading, tracing the mask's oversize head, its wide-flowing palm-leaf skirts. He noted the mask's provenance, the date, the name of the dead man it was created for. Luke had started the rice, and the starchy smell made Stephen hungry.

Luke nodded as Stephen pulled out a sketch he had made of a drum he'd bought the day before. He'd sketched the drum's full curves, its narrow chiseled waist, the taut snakeskin cover glued on with a paste of human blood and lime powder. The houseboy pointed at Stephen's drawing of the drum.

"Very good." Luke nodded. "Very good picture."

Luke smelled of jasmine oil and woodsmoke and sweat. Stephen looked back down at his notebook and began writing. He looked from his drawing of the spirit mask to the mask itself, propped between two duffel bags to keep it from being crushed. He tried to imagine it back in New York, behind glass, lit up, hanging on a freshly painted gallery wall. At that moment the mask seemed like a living creature. The idea of it strung up, dangling, in a museum was freakish.

Stephen had begun to feel at moments that what he was doing here was worse than Father Dougherty's Jesus preaching—all this collecting and note-taking and photographing and preparing for the grand exhibit in New York. He was about to expose the Asmat to the industrialized world in a way they couldn't conceive; he would hold them up to be examined and giggled over like a sliced-open frog pinned to the black-waxed bottom of a dissection tray.

His mind wandered out of the hut, around the village, down to the river. The grim certainty of failure had slipped into him like a virus, cloaking itself as worry that the art he was collecting was mediocre or the unshakable feeling that he was in over his head. That he couldn't understand much less exhibit this work. Or that the art was too primitive. Or just that he was ridiculous. A ridiculous, willful rich boy spending unearned money. Agitated, the night before, he'd flipped through the damp, tissue-thin pages of Father Dougherty's Bible, looking for passages he'd loved as a child. But, really, the Bible was only witchery, Stephen thought. It had no answers or comfort beyond its enveloping rhythms and the poetry of its images.

"Mister Stephen," Luke said, interrupting the swirl in Hesse's mind. "You want me to come with you on your trip?"

"Won't Father Dougherty miss you?" Stephen asked, surprised.

"Father Dougherty is okay. He said I can go with you."

"I don't know. I need to talk to Dr. Van Gropius."

Van Gropius had already hired two guides, but because Luke spoke English, because the priest had already trained him as an anthropological informant, he was as valuable as six guides. This was a lucky break, Stephen thought, but it unsettled him. Maybe it was too lucky? Was the priest sending Luke along as a spy?

"Have you really asked Father Dougherty?"

"Yes. Yes. He is very happy for me to help you." There was a long pause. Finally Luke said, "For my pay?"

Stephen had forgotten the eternal Asmat bargaining. It was not greed, this unquenchable thirst for spiced tobacco, beads, clothes, salt, rice, tinned fish and meat, Father Dougherty had explained to him. Balance was the central tenet of the Asmat worldview. Nothing is given without receiving. Nothing is taken without giving: not life, property, wives, work, food—nothing.

"How much *lempeng* does Father Dougherty give you for a day's work?"

"I do not smoke." Luke smiled.

"Oh," Stephen said, suspicious. "Knives?"

Luke shook his head.

"I want to see America," he said slowly, pronouncing the words perfectly. "Can you take me there, please?"

Stephen stared at Luke. He opened his mouth to speak and then closed it. He felt as though a bird had rushed into his hands, soft and warm, its heart thumping and beating in his palms. He didn't, wouldn't ever, even for a half-second, consider taking Luke anywhere. But he could see the New Guinean man so clearly: his tentative hope, his trying not to hope, his courage, his ambition. It was awful and intimate to see him, and Stephen closed his eyes, willing the connection between them to break. When he opened them again, he looked down at the houseboy's bare feet, strong and wide, splattered with mud, toes splayed.

"I'm not sure, Luke." Stephen was shaking his head, nervous. "It's so far away. You can't imagine how far away America is from Irma village."

"Father Dougherty told me America is far away. He said it costs great money to get there," Luke offered.

"Yes." Stephen nodded, bemused. "That, too."

"So, you are the only one who can take me. Your papa has the most money of all the white men. You," he said, "*you* can take me to America."

Slowly the blur in front of Stephen came into focus. He saw the whole thing then, as if he'd been there: the priest, threatened by the arrival of other white men, of a wealthy white man, had told his houseboy exactly who their visitors would be. The priest would have spit about evil moneybags in the shape of a white man on his way from Agats, warning Luke. And Luke, far ahead of the priest, had cooked up a scheme.

"Is that what Father Dougherty told you?"

Luke shrugged his shoulders.

Was it only ever the money? Was that the beginning and end of every story? All of a sudden Stephen was revolted by the priest's neat little hut, by his possessions. He saw himself, as though his spirit had left his body and stood watching his physical self. Blundering, grasping, buying, buying, buying, like a fat man gobbling pies at an eating contest.

Stephen looked at Luke. Looked into his brown-yellow eyes and the dark velvet black of his pupils. The houseboy deflated. His expression became narrow and closed.

Vanity of vanities, Stephen thought. All is vanity.

"Maybe we can go to America together someday," Stephen said. "But for this trip I'll pay you with knives, tinned fish, salt and matches, yes?"

Luke nodded his head, knowing he was being lied to. Yes, he would come.

THE NEXT MORNING THEY LOADED UP THE BOAT. THE CRANKY eighteen-horsepower outboard motor started up *put-put-put* and then it was chugging, humming, choking petrol smoke into the mist that sat on top of the still river. Van Gropius and Stephen had nailed a square of corrugated aluminum on top of two dugout canoes and bound them into a catamaran. The boat was packed with all their belongings: food, Van Gropius's whiskey, the extra petrol and two bags of rice Father Dougherty had given them. Stephen could barely look at the priest, leaving Van Gropius to say all the good-byes and thank-yous.

Inadvertently, as they floated on the river that morning, they created a scene from an ancient Egyptian frieze: Luke kneeling at the back of the catamaran, his hand on the rudder, suddenly as protective and dangerous-looking as Anubis; Stephen, the young pharaoh, in the middle of the boat, sitting, leaning back on a duffel, gazing ahead; Van Gropius, in front of him, hunched over the unfolded map on his lap. And Roman Adziepe, Luke's cousin, standing on the bow, peering into the distance.

The priest and his flock, children, women, some of the older Irma men, watched them from the riverbank.

And then they were off. Irma and its American priest evaporated with the early-morning haze. They were, all four travelers, in tune with the motor as it chugged and the soft *slap* noise of the boat pushing through the water as it headed up into the jungle, into this place that was so green and hot and full of life.

# 13

## THE *BISJ*

THE JUNGLE INHALED THEM, PULLING THEIR WEIGHTED-DOWN
catamaran along the river, into the hot, slow-moving world
of the salt swamps. They careened into muddy banks at low tide
and the three of them jumped into the shallow, warm water and
pushed and pushed the heavy boat while Luke guided it back to
deeper water with his long iron-wood paddle. Stephen was overwhelmed with the tangled vines and the smell of the wet rain-
forested swamp and the branches that hung over the water,
dripping orchids. He felt a warm, thick slowness pumping
through his blood. They were only a few days' journey from
Akapi, a village where Van Gropius had found out that three,
maybe even five, *bisj* poles awaited them.

Stephen had spent hours in Irma studying Van Gropius's
black-and-white photographs of the *bisj*. Tall, like the Easter Island totem poles, Stephen thought, but thinner, more complex,

elegant carvings that each represented a newly dead soul, a soul that demanded to be avenged in blood.

They learned to turn off the outboard motor when the river narrowed, and Luke and Roman steered with long paddles until the banks opened up wide enough, deep enough, to start the motor.

T'aint I, Huckleberry Finn? Stephen smiled to himself as he lay back on his duffel, lazy from the heat, and watched the mangroves and nipa palms slide by. Crocodiles rose up and broke the surface; ugly monsters, powerful, graceful as they glided alongside the catamaran, eyeballing the four of them and then submerging again.

> Oh, the little cargo-boats that sail the wet seas roun'
> They're just the same as you'n me a-plyin' up an' down

Stephen thought that he too was slipping away, like the crocodiles. It was only his old skin that sat in the boat, checking camera equipment and chatting with Van Gropius.

"WHAT ARE YOU ALWAYS SCRIBBLING AWAY AT?" VAN GROPIUS ASKED that night. They were camped in a rest house thirteen miles downriver from Akapi.

"A letter to my father."

"Oh yah? That's some letter. I thought maybe a diary."

"No." Stephen smiled, covering over his annoyance at the interruption, willing Van Gropius not to go on.

*Will I always remember this?* he wrote. Would he always be able to conjure the feeling of being in the jungle, the physicality of it? He worried that this time would become as fugitive as a dream. How impossible America seemed from here. But still, he could feel it burning away like the unseen sun that lit up the other half of the globe while New Guinea floated in blue night.

*I would like to live in the Asmat for a while,* he wrote. But then, even as he wrote it, he knew he'd never come back. Not to stay, not to live here. He envied Father Dougherty's freedom to send the rest of the world to hell. Stephen stopped writing. What *would* he do? he wondered. A part of him knew that New Guinea, even graduate school, would only buy a few years before he had to reckon with his life, his real life.

It wasn't meant for him to be a gentleman-scholar, he knew it even before he went to see Adams in Cambridge. Sometimes he had visions of himself, believable fantasies of the future— himself near the helm of the Hesse fortune, learning, working, helping control the gushing rivers of Hesse oil. And Sheila? She would never be his—he knew that. He would never have her; really, he never did. It made him sorry, but that night in the rest house thirteen miles downriver from Akapi village, the thought didn't make him panic. He thought Sheila was evaporating from his heart.

Fate had dropped him on a wall between two lives, Stephen thought; he could see both but could not fully enter either of them. He wasn't English or working-class, although his mother was; he wasn't a true child of the American super-rich, although his father was. He wasn't a Hesse like his stepbrothers, and he wasn't not a Hesse, either. He wasn't a scholar like John Nightingale, and he wouldn't even allow the wish to be a writer into his conscious mind. But a businessman? It seemed like a lifeless life to him. He would change, though. He would learn it all. He would be his father's son.

Stephen shook his head. He didn't want to think anymore. Instead, he looked over at Luke. Stephen had brought *Breakfast at Tiffany's* to the Asmat and hadn't been able to read it. Each page put him back in New York. And New York was only Sheila. Back in Irma village, Luke had asked to borrow the book to practice reading English. Stephen watched him now, poring over the pages of Capote's novel by the light of the kerosene lamp, underlining words he would ask Stephen about in the boat the next day.

Luke had a quality of loneliness about him that was so familiar. Father Dougherty's houseboy was an only child, too, an only son. Stephen was sad looking at Luke, and then he was feeling too much and his eyes welled up.

"You miss your family?" Van Gropius asked.

Stephen looked over at the Dutchman, uncomprehending. He was tumbling through his thoughts. Van Gropius was sitting on his sleeping bag, smoking a cigarette, smiling, his upper lip hidden by his dark mustache. The outside night had slipped inside through the rest house's thin woven-bamboo walls. The crickets and frogs were loud, the smell of the brackish mud strong in the cool, sticky air. Stephen stared at Van Gropius. He couldn't speak; he could not remember his family. For an instant, for half of a flash of a second, he was only himself, his true nameless self; he couldn't conjure Nicholas or Marguerite out of the Asmat night.

Mistaking Stephen's silence for homesickness, Van Gropius leaned over and put his hand on Hesse's shoulder.

"Well," the Dutchman said, "you'll see them for Christmas if the monsoon can control herself. Otherwise we'll be celebrating in Agats with the jungle rats who come to visit their town cousins for the holidays!"

AT HIGH TIDE, THE ARAFURA FLUSHED INLAND AND DEPOSITED the life that crawled along its bottom into the rivers that criss-crossed the swampy flatlands. Luke and Roman plucked saltwater shrimp from the river and boiled them. The four travelers ate the delicious pink, fleshy creatures on top of rice, salty from the sea. They caught crabs one time, crayfish another. Otherwise, every night Luke cooked rice and Spam and made hot tea. Breakfast was rice and tea. Lunch was rice and tinned mackerel.

They did not wash their bodies except when the rain fell and drip-dropped on their faces. Stephen's beard grew. He smelled musky and rank. He didn't sleep for more than a few hours a night, from the noise of the jungle and the mosquitoes and his own racing mind.

*I am in a place,* he wrote, *where people can't, or rather haven't yet, mastered nature; the rain, the moon, the animals and insects flex their power over us. I am a part of the world. Just that and no more and it may surprise you but I am so glad of it.*

THEY MADE THEIR WAY SLOWLY, TRAVELING FOUR MILES OR SO PER day. During the long, hot hours chugging along toward Akapi, Van Gropius worried out loud about the Indonesians.

"There's no Solomon to settle the squabble this time," he said. "The U.N. isn't interested, no? Nobody cares."

"What do you think the Indonesians'll do?" asked Stephen, trying to be polite. He figured he must be the only white man for a thousand miles not interested in this topic.

"Even your friend that cranky old priest—he's just as worried as anyone. Jesus won't save him from Jakarta and he knows it." Van Gropius shook his head. "There's nothing here—no

gold, hardly any oil, no coal. It costs many many millions of dollars every year just to run the bloody place."

So, Stephen thought, why not let it go? But he had understood it when he landed in Hollandia a month ago. The Dutch
were wrestling with their own possessiveness, as strong and
deadly as a mother's for her baby: western Netherlands New
Guinea was theirs, their own country. It was as though the Indonesians were scaling the nursery wall in full daylight preparing to steal the child and take it away forever. Well, Stephen
thought, let them have it! Why not give the Indonesians the
headaches of being a colonial government?

"What about going someplace else?" Stephen asked. "What
about South America?"

"Yah, yah," Van Gropius said. "Why aren't you in South
America following in the great Claude Lévi-Strauss's footsteps?"

"You know," Stephen said, giving the Dutch anthropologist a
hard look, "there isn't anywhere that you can go anymore that
you won't be facing the same problems that are here, Erich. But
it doesn't mean that the going isn't worth it."

"No, no. I know the world I was born into is gone. There's
nothing now but to go with this newness, this new ugly world,
and see where it will take us, yah?"


AS THEY APPROACHED AKAPI, A BAD FEELING SURFACED BETWEEN
Hesse and Van Gropius while they were discussing their itiner-
ary.

"After Akapi, I think we should head back for the coast,
maybe go to Rutanabe, which is more or less on the way back to
Agats."

"No," Stephen said. "We planned to visit at least three more villages before we turn around."

"Okay, Stephen. Sometimes you have to obey the weather in this part of the world, you know? This monsoon is coming earlier than I thought."

Stephen shook out the map on his lap and studied it intently. Finally: "Kisa and Laewae are only a day upriver from Akapi."

"No, not really. I think maybe more like two days to get up there and two to get back."

"The boat can go faster. We're not anywhere near the speed capacity of this motor."

"I don't think it's a good idea."

"Well. I really want to. It's what we agreed upon."

It amazed Van Gropius—the boy had never been here, never experienced a coastal monsoon, never stumbled upon a head-hunting raid in action. And he could say what they would do because he'd bought Van Gropius as much as Luke and Roman and the boat. The anthropologist fell into a sour mood and sat pouting as the boat kept motoring upriver. They would turn around, Van Gropius thought, and head for the coast, no matter what Stephen Hesse wanted. He refused to get stuck in an Asmat village for weeks on end. But he didn't need to argue about it.

As for Stephen, as they got closer and closer to Akapi, he blotted the European man out of his mind. He turned to Luke and the jungle and the river and the rare blue sky. Streams of white clouds drifted overhead.

Unexpectedly, bits of Marguerite's favorite poems, the Wordsworth she had read out loud and then made him memorize, beset him.

*Continuous as the stars that shine*
*And twinkle on the milky way,*
*They stretched in never-ending line*
*Along the margin of the bay:*
*Ten thousand saw I at a glance,*
*Tossing their heads in sprightly dance.*

Did he miss his mother, then? But he couldn't find her any-where inside of himself.

A fleet of war canoes emerged from a bend in the river.

"Ah," Van Gropius said, "we are to get a royal welcome."

A dozen of the long dugout canoes appeared, paddled by men who were standing straight up in the narrow boats, dressed for battle; white limestone paste striped their dark bodies, feather crowns created magnificent haloes over their faces and carved seashells hooked through their septums made them into a flock of enormous birds of prey flying, skimming the water. They encircled the catamaran, the Akapi warriors drumming the sides of their canoes with their paddles, chanting a rhythmic, repetitive song, smiling for Stephen, who'd pulled out his Leica to snap photos of them.

Luke turned off the engine, and one of the Akapi men, re-splendent in his paint and feathers, gave a speech.

"He says to you, the whole village, the grandmothers and the babies too, are happy you come to Akapi," Luke explained. "They are glad you are here and they want some braided to-bacco."

They started up the motor and chugged to the shore with their escort paddling alongside them, chanting songs, engulfing the world with their deep-voiced singing. Then, as they got close to shore, Stephen saw the *bisj*. There were five of them staked alongside one another in the mud, standing in front of the village's long, rectangular men's house. The poles were enormously tall, taller than the houses, taller even than most of the trees that surrounded the human settlement.

Stephen stepped out of the catamaran into the water without waiting for Van Gropius and walked up the riverbank, past a cluster of small houses on stilts, toward the *bisj*.

He was followed by a trail of excited, shouting, whispering children, who reached out tentative fingers to touch him and then pulled them back, screaming. The poles were incredible: they were much, much more than anyone had told him. The black-and-white photographs of the Dutch collections and Father Dougherty's and Van Gropius's descriptions had not prepared him.

The *bisj* were wood poles, carved and painted with figures of men who stood one stacked on top of another, feet balancing on a head or head-to-head, like circus acrobats. Protruding from the male figures who stood at the top of the poles were enormous bellies, phallic shaped and filled with openwork carving of curled umbilical-type cords, which in turn had small male figures emerging from their tips.

They are life, Stephen thought, looking up at them. A pure expression of what it was to be a man: sexual, angry, full of remorse, sorry to be a creature that will die. Of all living things in the world, only man knows that someday he will die and time will go on without him. Father Dougherty wasn't wrong about God's Grace in this art. The *bisj,* Stephen thought, had Beauty. Not just beauty of form or color or the power of their immense size but Beauty itself.

Stephen was rapt: in one part of his mind, he was aware that

the Akapi villagers were staring at him as openly as he was staring at their ancestor poles. He felt Luke behind him, and
Roman, too, nervous to be in an enemy village. He saw Van
Gropius walking up from the river, along the muddy shore. But
none of it mattered. He only wanted to take in the *bisj.*

HE UNDERSTOOD THEN WHAT FATHER DOUGHERTY HAD TOLD HIM
about some of the administrators in the colonial government
who argued for forbidding and burning these carvings as part of
the campaign to stamp out head-hunting. The Dutch or even the
Indonesians couldn't hope to compete with the carvings for control over the Asmat. The *bisj* had visceral power, as intoxicating,
he thought, as the great cathedrals of Europe must have been to
the shoeless peasants who worshipped in them. That's what
it was. In the truest sense, the *bisj* were religious, and what
government can compete with belief? And his own belief?
How much less bloody, less violent, even less cannibalistic, he
thought, was the story of the God he believed in?

There was something here, too, something in these wood
carvings, something that reminded him of the violence and ecstasy and death and transcendence of the Christ story.

Stephen did believe in his God. He didn't believe in a
church—they were, he thought, foul, unholy things. Yet he knew
that God was in him, was in everything, in all of life. Even here,
most especially here, Stephen felt God. He felt Him more than
he ever had in this muddy, human core of life, in the mass of seawater and mud that the Asmat people lived and died in.

Van Gropius walked over to the poles and started to explain
their iconography to him. The Dutchman pointed to the hollow
at the bottom of the *bisj* where the head-hunted skulls were

placed, *had* been placed during the last feast, he reckoned, pointing to what looked like dried black blood on the wood. The *bisj* were made to satisfy the anger and need for revenge of the newly dead. A life for a life, since no one in the entire Asmat believed that there was such a thing as natural death—everyone was a victim of warfare or witchery.

The anthropologist walked around the poles, describing the stylistics of the carving, the regional peculiarities, the coloring, with the cool assuredness of a docent lecturing at the Rijksmuseum on a Sunday afternoon.

STEPHEN BOUGHT THE FIVE *BISJ* POLES WITHOUT NEGOTIATING, unloading almost all of their trade goods on the Akapi. He also bought a soul canoe—an exquisitely carved piece, almost as long as a real Asmat canoe but too narrow for a man to stand in. The soul canoe carried six seats that were carved representations of hunched-over spirits facing an elaborate magical turtle that sat in the middle of the boat.

"What is this?" Stephen asked after he bought it. "It's unbelievable!"

"Incredible, no? Soul canoes are made for male initiation ritual. You see this?" Van Gropius pointed to the carved spirits' flat backs. "These are seats for the male initiates. They come out of the men's house and one boy sits on one spirit, like so, on a bench."

"And the turtle?"

Van Gropius touched the carved turtle, festooned with Job's-tears necklaces and feather earrings.

"The turtle is a symbol for fertility. See, a boy sits on the turtle and he hopes to be able to father many babies."

Stephen also bought masks, shields, kina-shell necklaces, even a series of toy bows and arrows.

"See, Erich. They were all wrong in the States. Everyone said that this area had been ravaged long ago by the Dutch collectors. But look, there is still so much fabulous stuff here!"

"Yah, I think so." Van Gropius was cool, still ruffled from their argument in the boat. And irritated, too, that Stephen seemed to have completely forgotten about it. He was so happy with his buying.

"I mean, don't you really, really think we've got amazing stuff? It's authentic. And so amazing. I never thought I would see anything like this."

"I think so. I think you have some truly good pieces now."

THE NIGHT STEPHEN BOUGHT THE *BISJ* POLES AND THE SOUL canoe he didn't write in his letter. Instead, he lay still as a rock in his sleeping bag, under the mosquito netting, sandwiched between Roman and Van Gropius. The four of them were staying in yet another tiny government rest house built for Dutch patrol officers. Stephen willed his mind not to roam outside around the five *bisj* or to thoughts of the exhibit at the Hesse Museum that was now inevitable.

Earlier, Van Gropius had given him a cup of whiskey and cooled boiled water to celebrate.

"Thank you," Stephen said, nodding his head to the older man while they drank. "Thank you for arranging all this."

Van Gropius shrugged his shoulders. "You are kind," he had said, and then laughed a small, modest laugh.

But still, a bitter feeling lingered between the two of them. The whiskey was good, though, warm in his throat and belly. It helped Stephen blot out the ghosts in his head and fill himself up with where he was. He wished he *were* a rock—or any object that only absorbed but didn't think or know or feel anything.

He listened to the sounds of Akapi village settling into the night: the singing and chanting from the men's house, layered over with women talking and babies crying, a woman shouting at a child. He breathed in the familiar smell of brackish mud and woodsmoke and wet bamboo.

Eventually, everything quieted down except for the singing, which went on deep into the night, stopping and then starting up again. Stephen followed the rhythm of the Akapi songs, the moaning sounds, the coy invitation, the wild loneliness of the muddy river flowing through the salt swamps.

# 14

## TO THE COAST

THE NEXT MORNING, STEPHEN AGREED TO CUT THE TRIP SHORT. He was so occupied with the *bisj* poles and repelled by the undertone of true anger in Van Gropius's insistence that he didn't argue. They packed up the catamaran, bringing with them most of the smaller pieces that Stephen had bought. The *bisj* and the other large carvings were going to be brought to Agats later by a few Akapi men Stephen had hired for the task.

Van Gropius continued fretting about the monsoon, searching the haze-filled sky as though it might change from minute to minute. He grumbled and complained as he loaded up the catamaran. They could have avoided this situation if Stephen had listened to him. Now they were in a real rush. Now Van Gropius was worried, he said; yes, he was very concerned, and irritated too, that he'd hurried out of Agats before he could get them a two-way radio.

The catamaran was heavy, weighed down with cameras, film, recording equipment, small sculptures and field notes—uneaten bags of rice and tinned meat, the first-aid box, their clothes and dozens of the smaller artifacts. All of it made the lashed-together canoes sluggish in the water. The little boat and its outboard motor were put upon in a way that they had not been when they left Irma.

Thoughts and urges flitted through Stephen as they packed and got ready to leave. He wished he had his copy of *Tristes Tropiques*. Memories of Sheila intruded on him. In his head, he started a letter to John Nightingale. He had meant to write it in New York, but he hadn't been able to. He wished John were with him right then, helping him see this as an adventure, see the humor in Van Gropius's relentless gloom. But the more Stephen tried to figure out the way to make it right between him and John, the worse he felt. He didn't have any idea what to write.

Akapi tribesmen accompanied the catamaran downriver for a while, chanting as they paddled through the light morning rain. Stephen took the Leica out of his rucksack and photographed the warriors standing in their long, thin dugout canoes against the green tangle on the shore. Even though the Akapi men were not in the full battle dress they had worn to greet the art collectors, they looked stronger and more beautiful to Stephen than when he had first seen them; that morning they were like figures gliding through a dream. A weird feeling of regret passed through him when the Akapi turned their boats around and paddled away.

But then Stephen was distracted by the allure of the river. He took photo after photo on their way to the sea. The trees and vines along the riverbank emerged, twisting green and black, through the diffuse light. Flocks of sparrows flew overhead from one tree to another. Catfish swam just under the surface of the brown water. How could he not take all these photographs?

He began writing in his head; everything else—the other men in the boat, the sound of the outboard motor, the puddle of cold water he sat in—had retreated to the corners of his awareness. He felt like he was swimming through the river, tasting and seeing and smelling this place as though he were only his soul, submerged in the warm, life-filled water. He thought about building a hut near this shore and living like a holy hermit for a year, rid of language, able to experience life sensually, with no distraction.

THE RAIN WAS SOFT AND THERE WAS NO WIND, BUT THEY WERE IN the storm. Luke and Roman and Van Gropius recognized it.

Although the drizzle stopped by the time they motored into the mouth of the river, the three men were very nervous. The monsoon was gathering its force, waiting for just a moment at the top of its breath before it would explode onto the Casuarina Coast. The sun blared behind moisture-heavy clouds. The sea was already rough. Luke looked worriedly at Stephen, at the sky, at his cousin.

"The monsoon is here, Stephen," Van Gropius said, interrupting the silence.

Stephen looked out at the river, which had become a gushing, powerful force as it emptied itself into the coastal sea.

"But it's not *here* here. Not yet," Stephen said. "Can't we still get to Agats by this afternoon? Isn't that our plan, Erich?"

The Dutchman was silent and Stephen continued his prodding. "All we need to do is cut out across the bay instead of hugging the coast, right? Isn't that the route the patrol officers use? Isn't that what having a motor does for us?"

Van Gropius nodded slowly. He didn't want to spend Christmas in Agats, either. Or another moment with Stephen Hesse that he didn't have to. But still. He didn't like what he saw. He had never been out on the water in this kind of weather. Although they only needed to get a short distance down the coast.

"Yes, I think we can go." He hesitated.

Roman and Luke were talking together.

"We're going now, gentlemen," Van Gropius boomed at them.

Luke looked at the Dutch anthropologist and pointed at the sky.

"We're cutting across the bay," he said. "We'll use the motor."

Van Gropius switched into Malay, urging, cajoling. The cousins' reluctance only seemed to encourage him to head for Agats. Later on, Luke would think that Van Gropius had made his decision in anger. How could any man who had experienced the seasonal rains on this coast have headed out that day?

"Do you think we should offer them more pay?" Stephen asked Van Gropius. "I'll be happy to double or triple it."

Stephen was thinking that the coastal water didn't look that forbidding. He'd sailed through much worse up in Maine. Van Gropius was only protecting himself, Stephen thought, from criticism of not following the official Dutch government manual.

"Let's just go, Erich, tell them I'll double their pay."

"Oh no you don't. If you start renegotiating at this point, Stephen, then every single time you're in this part of the world, you will be open for manipulation. Not to mention the rest of us."

Stephen nodded. He still wanted to offer the cousins more money. But he kept quiet.

Luke and Roman didn't want to go. They had a choice: they could desert Hesse and Van Gropius, or they could stay and help them. Stephen Hesse and Erich Van Gropius were white men. They couldn't be stopped or reasoned with unless they wanted to be. And all three of them in the boat felt the full force of Stephen's restlessness and power. He wanted to go, go, go. In the end, none of them could resist his will.

Luke steered the catamaran hesitantly through the murky water, out of the river's mouth, and headed south into the bay, away from the coast. Tangled-up mangrove branches and roots and nipa-palm leaves spit out by the river floated in the ocean waves. The catamaran bounced, hard, in the chop. The rain started again, but it was still a soft, drizzling preamble to the storm.

And then, in less than a minute, white-capped waves swamped the engine. The catamaran began to drift, bobbing up and down in the churning water. Without the engine's constant rumble, the quiet became enormous and terrifying.

The four of them were alone together while their boat rocked on the wide sea. Not one of the men in the boat could believe yet what was happening in front of them.

# BOOK 4

*And there is time for you to change your mind—*

*Do you need further proof that you are mine?*

—OVID, *METAMORPHOSES*, BOOK 11

# 15

## THE *PIETÀ*

S TEPHEN HESSE'S SOUL ROAMED AROUND NEW YORK FOR MORE than a month after he disappeared into the Arafura Sea. He visited his father and Marguerite when they lay sleeping and in the midst of their days. He hovered over Sheila, blocking out the light in her painting studio so she couldn't think or work. He haunted Kiki and each of her children.

He haunted John Nightingale, who drove down from Cambridge to Haleyville for the memorial but in the end couldn't go into Hesse Chapel and sat in his car, in the cold, smoking, feeling sorry. Even Jane Lyle felt Stephen's spirit that day as it rushed into the chapel on a gust of wet December wind.

He haunted Billy Chadwick, who sat at the back of the small stone church, surrounded by his and Stephen's old teachers and schoolmates from Bromley and some of the guys from the Fly, Stephen's club at Harvard. Chadwick's gaze drifted from the glowing stained glass to the mass of blond children in black fidgeting in the front pews to the governor, ramrod-straight next to his second wife.

Billy listened to the minister, really listened, and tried to understand him—*Ask and it shall be given you; seek and ye shall find; knock and it shall be opened unto you. For everyone that asks receives; and he that seeks finds; and to him that knocks it shall be opened*—wondering why it was that he could not feel anything for his friend yet.

STEPHEN'S SPIRIT NAGGED AT HIS FATHER, SOMETIMES APPEARING as a child, sometimes as his grown self. He followed Nicholas everywhere, sliding under his skin, floating in his mind, distracting the governor from the work of the day, from his other thoughts. All his life Nicholas had had a sense of not being the same age in his heart as he was in his body. He felt—not young, but not old either, just that he was himself as he'd always been. Now, though, he knew that he had finally grown into his age. His quick, sensual feel for people, for ideas, had dulled and would crumble away in the years before he died. He had lost his son for no reason at all.

IT WAS IN THOSE FIRST FEW WEEKS AFTER STEPHEN'S MEMORIAL that the ghoulish fantasy that he'd been killed, cooked and eaten by the Asmat people appeared in the popular press. The tale grew details, and over time split into endless variations with names and facts and colorful embellishments. The gruesome story, like the fact of Stephen's death, would never go away; it outlived the governor and Marguerite. In time the story that

Stephen had been eaten by cannibals would outlive anyone who had ever known him.

Nicholas Hesse strode across the gleaming black marble lobby of 1062 Park Avenue and rode the A-tower elevator up to his first wife's apartment. He had not been in the elevator, in the A tower, in the place where his son grew up, in twenty years. He closed his eyes. What if he were on his way to see Stephen? I am that father whom your boyhood lacked and suffered pain for the lack of. I am he.

Marguerite opened her door, and the yellow entranceway, covered in the same wallpaper she had picked out when they'd first moved in from England, spread behind her. The faint smell of lavender and stale cigarette smoke floated out of the apartment. She was slow and drugged. Her eyes were red rimmed, her face swollen.

"Marguerite," Nicholas said, tasting her beautiful name in his mouth. "I wanted to see how you were doing."

His first wife looked at him, her brown eyes blank. She didn't ask him in; she didn't say a word. She only stood there watching him. Marguerite knew that he wasn't a stranger, but she hadn't recognized him yet.

The governor began to weep, and still she was unmoved. She wouldn't reach out her hand; she wouldn't touch him.

"I didn't understand," he said, and took off his glasses. He wiped his tears with his pocket handkerchief, shaking his head side to side: *no, no, no.* "I never really understood how hard it was on the two of you. I didn't know, Marguerite, I didn't know."

Marguerite emerged from under her narcotic haze. She glared at him.

"I'm so sorry," he said. "I'm so sorry about our boy. About everything."

She couldn't look at him anymore. She stared down at the floor. They stood like that, the two of them, suffering. Marguerite would not give him anything. She turned her back on her husband (he would always be her husband) and closed the door, leaving Nicholas in the hallway, staring after her.

FOR WEEKS STEPHEN INHABITED THE HONEY LOCUSTS THAT FRINGE Central Park, the traffic lights as they flashed green to gold to red. He passed through the bodies of other young men; he hovered over the city, weeping soft, cold snowflakes and icy, hard rain.

Gradually, his soul drifted away, sometimes reappearing, startling Sheila or Chadwick or even Gwathmey and Professor Adams, or Mrs. Lyle as she walked to work. And up in Connecticut at the Bromley School, the young classical-languages teacher, Christopher MacNeice, stumbled out of the novel he wrote on the weekends when Stephen's shadow crossed his desk. *Deficit omne quod nascitur.* But, mostly, Stephen was gone.

Except that, just like his own father, he couldn't really leave Marguerite, not completely. And it was hard for her, it was so hard for her to be left, but not really, only half left, first by her husband and then by her son. She screamed in the middle of empty night, pulled out of deep, sedated sleep by the vision of Stephen drowning. So she drugged herself completely, plugging the holes and cracks of her mind. She stayed inside the apartment at 1062 Park Avenue for eight months, floating in a sea of pills, days and nights full of pills, the metallic taste of induced sleep in her mouth.

Marguerite hardly moved. She hardly ate; she rarely moved her bowels. But sometimes the Valium and Seconal didn't work and she was up all night, smoking, wandering from room to room, agitated, so alone but invaded, too, by her life, by her son, by her mother, by her husband. Her too-big apartment was desolate at night, much worse than during the day. Gloom filled the rooms, robbing them of any joy or beauty they might have once contained. She mulled over her past ceaselessly, working it into tatters.

IT HAD STARTED THE SEPTEMBER WHEN MARGUERITE RETURNED from England after her own mother had died. Stephen began the retreat from her that would last the rest of his life. It had broken her heart when she felt her son regarding her under hooded eyes.

"What is it, lovey?" she would plead with him.

But he only ever shook his head. "Nothing, Mummy," and looked back at her with her own brown eyes.

He hacked at the ties that bound the two of them, that had grown as strong as the beards that shoot out from mussels' lips and cling to their rocky tidal beds. She was helpless to stop him. The closer she moved in, the farther he stepped away, leaving for boarding school, for college, for New Guinea.

Yet he kept his home with her; his room was full of his clothes and books; his mail all came to her apartment. He spent his summers with her in Maine, although he began visiting Kiki's house when his father was there. At Harvard he always came home to her for the holidays. Whether this was his choice or because Kiki did not want him in her realm, Marguerite didn't know, didn't want to know. It was enough for her that even when her son became cold and distant, his eyes full of disapproval, he was still hers.

AFTER STEPHEN DISAPPEARED IN NEW GUINEA, MARGUERITE couldn't employ a housekeeper. Walking inside her apartment fresh from outside was like entering the underworld. The sour smell of grief and age had permeated the furniture, the thick pile carpeting, the maid's room off the kitchen, the walls and paintings and towels in the bathrooms.

No one wanted to work for Mrs. Hesse. One after another they left after a few weeks of her unopened windows, unwashed bed linen, the dirty clothes she shoved to the back of her closets. She spent days in bed reading, the way she had as a girl. Stacks and stacks of books and papers and unanswerable mail filled up her bedroom, and the mess wasn't at all uncomfortable to her.

Eventually, she hired a housekeeper, named Iris, who stayed. Iris was Hungarian, an enormously overweight young woman, not even twenty when she started working at 1062.

She wore wide cotton housedresses, printed with poinsettias or purple chrysanthemums, that showed off her arms: her huge arms, pink, freckled, dimpled with fat. It seemed impossible to Marguerite that the woman could get around New York City, much less cook and clean the immense apartment, but she did it all.

Iris was unafraid of the Hesse name, of the death-filled feeling in the apartment. Unafraid of the suffocating wealth. The housekeeper threw open the windows and let cross-breezes flow through the apartment, carrying in the smell of fresh, wet city air. Slowly, meticulously, she fished months' worth of the dirty clothes from the back of Marguerite's closets. She washed everything. She ordered meat from the butcher on Madison Avenue and put in a standing order at the florist for weekly deliveries.

Marguerite never saw Iris eat anything except for the foil-wrapped butterscotch candies she kept in her purse. But how she cooked: delicious Hungarian stews and soups, thick cinnamon-cream rice pudding, pink apple sauce, paprika-and-yogurt chicken.

Iris stayed and brought life with her. Her radio played in the kitchen: kind male voices murmuring the news, advertisements for cough syrup and new restaurants. The housekeeper packed up Stephen's room, carefully wrapping up his possessions and putting mothballs in the trunks with his clothing and blankets and towels. She ordered slipcovers from Lord & Taylor, and eventually it could pass for an unused guest bedroom.

IN 1964, WHEN STEPHEN O'KEEFE HESSE WAS DECLARED LEGALLY, officially, dead, it was Iris who held Marguerite when she got the certified copy of his death certificate. She yelled that she would tear her hair out, scratch the skin off her body, cut herself until she bled rivers down her legs and arms; she cursed her own birth, her mother, Nicholas. She wished death on all of Kiki's children.

Finally, Iris let go and Marguerite slumped down to her housekeeper's feet, hunched over, shuddering, her broken heart spilling all over the kitchen floor.

"Ah, my dear," Iris murmured, stroking Marguerite's white curls. "You'll see your boy in the sweet hereafter."

But Marguerite couldn't be comforted. She knew her son was gone forever. Marguerite was still, after all this time, an intellectual woman, an armchair literary critic, who had spent her quiet, lonely adult life reading serious books. She had grappled with Sartre, Joyce and Beckett; she drank *The Second Sex,* Lawrence's novels, *Justine* and *Balthazar; The Sheltering Sky.* Although she liked to read Saint Catherine of Sienna's letters, she didn't—she hadn't ever (even when she tried)—believe in God or the sweet hereafter; heaven or hell. She knew that there is only this life. And that the human soul is as mortal as an earthworm.

After Stephen was declared legally dead, Iris moved in and hired a cleaning woman to help her. Iris cooked delicious meat pies and pastries but nothing ever too savory, never too spicy or sweet. She drew Marguerite baths of steaming-hot water and sprinkled Epsom salts into the tub; took her to the doctor, gave her her sleeping pills and brushed out her hair in the evening.

Eventually, Marguerite went out of the apartment by herself. She walked through Central Park, dead to the flowers and trees, to the winter snow covering the small hills.

She got lost in her reveries and wandered for hours in the park, around the reservoir, following the footpaths wherever they took her. In the warm weather she brought books with her, poetry mostly: Wordsworth and Shelley, Keats and T. S. Eliot, Rupert Brooke. How she had loved Rupert Brooke as a girl. And Eliot and his Prufrock—how could so much time have passed and his words were still arranged on the page just the same as they had always been?

She had loved those poets when she was twenty and she loved them now. She murmured her favorites and recited to herself what she knew by heart, as she had in the past to her mother, her husband, her son.

*I gazed—and gazed—but little thought*
*What wealth the show to me had brought*
*For oft when on my couch I lie*
*In vacant or in pensive mood,*

*They flash upon that inward eye*
*Which is the bliss of solitude;*
*And then my heart with pleasure fills,*
*And dances with the daffodils.*

These were the moments when Marguerite Hesse forgot her life and floated in an unknowing consciousness. Then she would feel Stephen there, sitting with her on the park bench, conjured by the sunlight and the quiet and the green park until she reached for him, and then he was gone, weightless as the wind. And so she would pick it all back up, every minute of her life, like a woman resuming knitting after stopping for a moment to watch a bird on the wing cross the sky.

SHE LOOKED OUT AT THE CITY FROM HER APARTMENT. THE traffic, the buses, the taxis, housemaids, people walking their dogs, deliverymen, groups of schoolchildren walking toward Fifth Avenue.

Marguerite watched day after day as life unfolded silently beneath her thick windows. She floated out over New York, wishing she could dive in and recapture herself. But she would never do it. She would only ever wait up there, forever looking out the window, waiting for her son to come home, for her life to start up again, until it was much too late.

# 16

## ON A WIDE, WIDE SEA

SWIMMING NUDE FELT SO GOOD AT FIRST. EVEN AS HE STARTED to get exhausted from the waves bullying him, he still liked being naked in the water; it was warm and soft, tickling him. It was raining again, harder than before, the drops splashing on his face. He swam on, plowing through the waves, imagining the sea he swam above: rich, brimming with fish and slithering eels and the unseeing life of sponges and coral and fluttering anemones. He knew there were Wildcats and Japanese Zeroes underneath him, fighter planes that had lit into flames and smashed into these waves twenty years ago. They would be rusted out by now, sleeping on the sandy bottom, their hard edges softened by the sea.

Stephen stopped swimming and treaded water, bobbing in the waves. He looked behind him for Van Gropius: if he could see the Dutchman, he would swim back and admit defeat. But he couldn't find Van Gropius.

The silliest thing, Stephen thought, was how annoyingly thirsty he'd become. "I'm thirsty," he said out loud.

But now he couldn't find the coast, either. He must have gone in the wrong direction, or maybe the current had pulled him off his path. He looked up at the raining sky. Stephen knew that help would come from the air—he knew they'd send search planes when they realized he was missing. He wished he had swum for the coast with Luke and left Roman in the boat with Van Gropius.

Stephen set out again, but now he wasn't at all sure which direction he was moving in. For a while the difficult work of swimming kept him from panic. And he tried calling up memories, faces to distract himself. But then the cold, implacable idea that he was going to die entered his flesh, physically entered his soul, and the panic began. He swallowed huge mouthfuls of seawater before he could get control. He was nauseated by the saltwater and he was tired, but he was so strong—his heart was powerful. He was an athlete; this knowledge was in his body itself, in his muscles and blood, in his soul, as he kept smacking the water, his legs aching with exhaustion.

But the idea of death stayed with him. He didn't want to die! But here it was anyway: naked I came from my mother's womb and naked I shall return. And as he flapped and splashed like a frightened seal, he tried to think of his father, the two of them alone, praying together at the Haleyville chapel so long ago . . . but then he let the memory dissipate.

He willed his life out of his mind. Finally there was nothing.

His lungs began to burn. He had swallowed too much water. Here was the pain. His body had been waiting for it. He was suffocating, choking, trying to stay on top of the waves with all his strength, with every cell in his body. All of him wanted life. But blackness came and released him. As his brain began to shut down, as he sank slowly through the upper layers of the sea, his life, his memories, left him; but from the deepest core of his being a warm tingling flushed through him, a delicious, ecstatic moment of joy.

His dying brain reached out to God, who was swimming next to him, bathing him in His golden light.

But it wasn't God. It was only life, life itself fluttering free of his limbs and leaving in its wake diminishing electrical currents. Soon, the unknowing body of Stephen Hesse sank down into the sea.

# ACKNOWLEDGMENTS

I would like to thank Duncan Bock for the generous gift of his insight, acuity and guidance.

I would also like to thank Lee Boudreaux, Sloan Harris, Jhumpa Lahiri and James Rahn for their invaluable help.

And *vade in pace* to Michael Clark Rockefeller, art collector, photographer, visionary and Student of Man.

```
============================================

        Loyalty Points Award
         05/17/2014 17:05
           Member 700346
           Rioux, Martha
============================================


Eligible Amount: $ 4.00
 Current Points: 4
 Points Balance: 258



         Thank you!
--------------------------------------------
```

## ABOUT THE AUTHOR

SAMANTHA GILLISON is the author of *The Undiscovered Country,* which was nominated for the *Los Angeles Times* Art Seidenbaum Award and was named a *Los Angeles Times* Book of the Year. She has won a Whiting Fiction Award and a 2003 Guggenheim Fellowship. She lives in New York City.